Binding of the Almatraek

Book One:

Knight's Surrender

Written By

Heather Reilly

Published by Reilly Books
ISBN-13: 978-0991936700
ISBN-10: 0991936701

Acknowledgments

I would like to thank, both from the bottom of my heart and the bottom of my cup, the staff at the Brant Street Second Cup in Burlington, Ontario. Illsurn runs a beautiful place, and she as well as Nicole, Mark, and her other wonderful staff created a space where I could write and drink spectacular caramelo coffee, and bring the world of Endalwynndale to life. This book was almost completely written at this location, and I am very grateful for their attention, service, and for allowing me to occupy their tables for hours on end.

I would also like to thank my editors. You gave me insight from outside the window looking in, that I would have missed on my own. Thank you also for your encouragement from the very first draft.

Other books by the author:

Binding of the Almatraek
Book II: Noble Pursuit

The Tree and the Sun

Upcoming Books:

Binding of the Almatraek
Book III: Enchanting Page

Tock Tick Tock!
The Mouse and the Clock

All titles are available at
www.reillybooks.com

This book is dedicated to my wonderful husband, who remains as magical as the journey that brought me here.

This book is also for my students, who taught me that the simple things in life can bring the greatest amount of joy, and that the little things mean a lot.

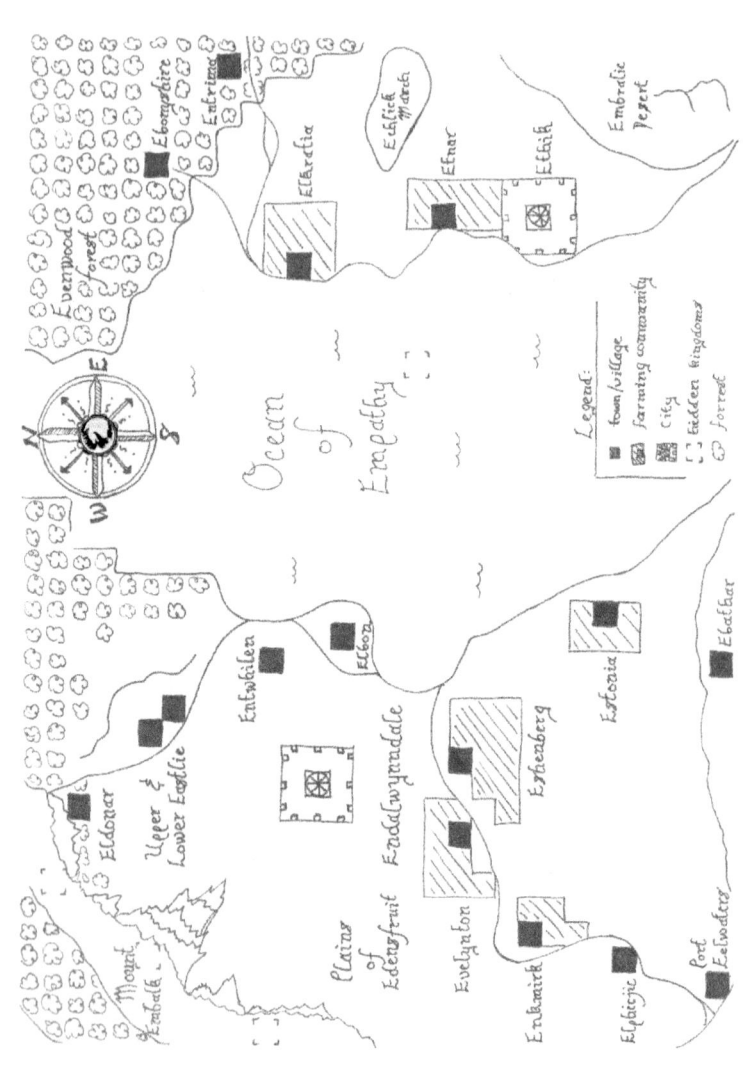

Chapter 1
~ Destiny ~

he ran. The nature scented breeze flipped up the ends of her page-cropped, blond hair as she pelted through the forest amid bird calls and wind-blown rustling leaves. Terrified, with her heart racing and the sound of her own measured breaths and the horse's heavy hooves coming to her ears, she tried to summon more speed to open the gap between them. She fumbled with the soft leather pouch that dangled from her belt, and extracted a pinch of fine yellow dust. As she ran, she forcefully threw it to the ground behind her, careful not to let any particles land on the backs of her deerskin shoes. As soon as the powder made contact with the path, the few leaves, ferns and twigs there burst into a mighty flame three feet high. The idea was to throw off the knight that was in hot pursuit by dazzling him, and not by scorching his horse. After all, the beast was in service to the knight and under his control whether it wished to be or not, much like the people of the kingdom he served. The smell was acrid and the quick pop and sizzle of the ignited twigs was enough to make the horse rear, buying her a few more precious seconds of a lead. Unfortunately, the determined knight remained in his saddle.

She could see the clearing up ahead where the trees thinned and let in the brilliant sunlight, and she poured on more speed. She broke through the last few pieces of brush, and felt the temperature change as she left the shade of the forest and entered the sunny fields that surrounded her home. The sun was warm on her face as she raced along the open path that led to the large village. The girl felt a surge of relief as she shot through the gates that marked the barrier to her family's property. She grasped the rough wooden gate post, and ignoring the sharp sting of a sliver that pierced her flesh, slammed the gate behind her, desperately hoping to slow the knight by another moment more. *Why does he chase me still,* she wondered in bewilderment as she ran, *I didn't do anything wrong, the fire didn't actually hurt anyone!* A painful stitch began to stab at her gut as she flew across her family's fields and boroughs, and she made a failing effort to adjust her rasping breathing to deeper, more even breaths. She smelled grass and stepped sure-footedly on the familiar dusty path until she reached a little cottage and vegetable garden bordered by a shorter wooden fence. She continued to run though the stitch had wormed its way deeper into her side, and her breath now only came in agonizing gasps. Finally, as her legs began to loosen into jelly under her, she smelled her mother's cooking wafting out her own windows, and she mustered the energy to close the distance to her front door.

She burst in, throwing herself over the threshold, and slammed the door behind her. She heard it latch, and ran to take refuge in the kitchen behind her mother's plump body. Blinded by the dim indoor light after being out in the bright sunshine, the smell of hearty stew enveloped her as she clutched the back of her mother's coarse skirt. "Whatever he says, Mother, trust that I didn't do it!" she panted desperately, trying to focus her wild eyes on the door as thundering hoof beats approached outside.

"What's all this about now?" her riled mother demanded, wondering what she was being asked to protect her child from. But in response, all she got was an ominous knocking at the door made with the forceful clanking of a metal gauntlet. "Oh by the shields of the army of Ormond, what have you done now child?" she complained, exasperated, shoulders slumping. Not really expecting an answer, the matron went to go open the heavy oak door.

As her mother shuffled toward the door, the girl looked frantically around the cottage for another place to hide. It was a small place, but tidy. Dishes that were stacked neatly on a shelf and pots and pans that hung from the wall beside the bright crackling hearth denoted the kitchen area. *Nowhere to hide there,* she thought in panic. Next to it, taking up much of the main room, was the big table complete with bench seats and clean table cloth. This space served as the family's dining area, and also offered nowhere to hide. The floor was wood in the sleeping area, but in the main room of the cottage, it was made of packed stone and dirt so that it was solid and level. This meant that there was no basement to run to. Then she remembered her bed. She ran under the dull brown curtain that hung by a wooden rod that marked the end of the main room and the beginning of the room behind it. Her shoes shuffled on the hidden room's wooden floor as she ran past her mother's large bed, and scuttled beneath her own narrow bed frame. This too, was made of wood and offered her just enough room to fit, though her blanket did not quite reach the floor.

From the other room, she heard her mother's gasp as the woman opened the door to reveal one of the king's own men. "I am Carn, of Endalwynndale, a knight in Ormond's army, and sworn protector of King Eurilas," he announced in a clear, commanding voice, "I seek the young girl."

"That'd be my daughter Sir, but please, whatever she's done-" She stopped mid-sentence as Carn's hand rose, palm out, to silence her.

"I must speak with the child," was his only reply.

Under the bed, the girl's palms had begun to sweat and she heard her own heartbeat thumping loudly in her ears. She wondered vaguely why he didn't hear its racing beat, and come to collect her at once. She gulped thickly as butterflies soared in her tummy, making her feel sick like the time she had accidently drank some milk that had gone bad. Resigned to the fact that her mother would be of no help to her, the girl blew out a breath that made the hair in her face fly up on the gust she had created. She wriggled out from under the bed and straightened, taking the time to set her clothes right. She brushed off some of the gritty dirt her clothes and sweaty palms had collected from the wooden floor, combed her fingers hurriedly through her hair, and tucked the front portion, too long to be called bangs, behind her ear.

It was thin, and was the same length all the way around, hanging just under her jaw line. She almost always wore her hair down, as it helped to hide her freckle-speckled cheeks and long lashes. She felt that they were at odds with each other: her eyes were probably her best feature, a deep turquoise blue, and the thick blonde lashes that framed them made them stand out. However, the multitude of freckles on her face made her look like she was much younger than her years, and made her feel about as unladylike as her figure. She was tall for a ten year old, standing just over five feet, one inch. She was neither fat nor thin, with sturdy arms and legs. In her opinion, she still had the curveless body shaped like a boy's from helping her mother with the farm chores, and her clothes hung loosely around her. Today she wore a tan tunic with navy trim, navy hose, and a thick brown leather belt round her waist to hold her pouches. She squared her shoulders, swallowed her fear, and walked out to meet her destiny.

o

Chapter 2
~ Tinder Toes ~

In the other room, the girl's mother had invited Carn to seat himself at the table while she presented him with a cool cup of water not too long from the well. She bustled around in her grey dress and white apron, curly blonde hair tied back into a makeshift bun as she worked. She hummed a sweet tune as she cut up some bread and sliced some rich cheese to set before him and worried, *If her highness doesn't get her buttocks out here soon, I'm soon going to have to go in after her!* It was on the heels of this thought that she heard the rustle of the curtain and she looked up to see that her only daughter had joined them in the room.

The girl stood awed now that she had time to actually stop and appreciate the appearance of the knight. He was clad neck to boot in bright silvery scale armour. He had removed his massive helm, which gleamed on the tabletop, striking, with its fringe of royal blue fur down the centre. He had removed his gauntlets, fur-lined in black with an insignia on the silver back. His cape was of the finest blue velvet, and it too was trimmed with more silver. He wore a sword that was so long that its scabbard brushed the floor as he sat, and she could see that the insignia of a dragon's head blowing fire on the hilt matched those on his gloves and chest plate. He too had blond hair, though his locks were thick and waved lazily to his shoulders. He had a serious brow and a stern jaw, and his eyes were of an icy blue that could have been gentle or merciless. Though he sat calmly now, the chase had left him sweaty which filled the room with a faint odour.

He studied the girl with an unfathomable look. "It seems there is nowhere else for you to run," he admonished, "You have wasted more than a bit of my time with this game of pursuit, young lady."

"Then you should have let me go," the girl replied hotly "I didn't do anything wrong!"

Gasping once again, the girl's mother scolded her, "I did not raise a daughter who would think to address their elders in such a way, and a knight of the king too, petulant child!"

But Carn chucked low in his chest, amused by the girl's feistiness. "I never said you were being detained because you did something wrong youngling, if that were the case, you'd have been run through in the market where you stood," he confessed. The girl felt her mouth go dry, and vainly struggled to swallow as he went on. "In truth, Prince Oslan saw your little performance and was intrigued, asking me to seek you out to share an audience with him." His armour clinked gently as he raised a bite of cheese to his mouth.

Shocked, the girl replied: "But I have done nothing to garner notice by the prince, I was just shopping in the marketplace, it was not my fault..." She let her voice trail off as she sullenly noticed that neither of the two adults in the room was buying her excuse.

"What exactly *did* happen?" the woman questioned. Though she spoke to the knight, she gave her girl a withering look. The girl groaned inwardly and allowed herself to plop down onto the bench across from the knight. Trying to disappear, she poured her concentration into digging the painful sliver from her palm.

"Your daughter," replied the knight amused, "did something very brave today. She spoke in truth of shopping in the marketplace, when she must have spied a man trying to make off with some goods at a nearby merchant's stall. She boldly walked up to him and said something to him, at which point his shoes mysteriously caught ablaze."

The girl sunk deeper in her seat and bowed her head lower at her mother's sharp gasp. *I'm really in for it this time,* she thought, the butterflies in her tummy again fluttering up a frenzy. To her surprise, Carn began to chuckle as he reassured her mother, and the girl timidly peeked out from behind her hair to watch him tell the rest of the story.

"Not to worry Madam, the scoundrel ran to the nearest horse trough and jumped in feet first to extinguish the flames. It was really quite amusing, and I can assure you that no one was hurt. In fact, the merchant asked me to offer this to her in gratitude," the knight added as he pulled from a pouch a bracelet braided from wiry white horse hair with two turquoise beads to match the girl's eyes. Her nervousness was replaced by wonder, and she extended a shaky hand to accept the treasure. "Let it remind you of your good deed done today," he advised as he placed the jewelry in her palm. "If you do not mind the enquiry, what exactly did you say to that poor old thief?"

The girl answered distractedly as she tried to fasten the bracelet round her wrist. "I had to distract him while I pulled out some powder, so I simply said: Sir, I think there maybe something wrong with your shoe! ˝ Much to her surprise, the charmed adults burst out laughing in the tiny kitchen, much as the prince had done from his vantage point that morning above the market in the castle window.

"I think it is time for you to come with me now to meet the prince," said Carn, "You should pack your bags and expect to stay a while, and bring your little pouch, it may be of use to you. I cannot tell you what the prince has in store for you at this point, but I know that he will be anxiously awaiting our arrival. What name should I give him so that I can introduce you properly?"

A rush of emotions ran through the girl. Panic, for one, as this man was trying to remove her from her home at but a moment's notice, but the royalty in this land was supposed to be good, so she did not fear meeting the prince. This would be like an adventure for sure, which brought with it excitement. However, there was also sadness that her happy life was about to change in one way or another. She felt guilt for surprising her mother with this unpleasantness, and she knew she would be leaving her only parent in a lurch, having yet to complete some of her chores. Finally, resigned, she decided that regardless of all that, Carn hadn't really given her a choice.

As she mulled all this over, she stood and absently made ready to pack her bag. Going into her bedroom, she put her few garments into a sack, along with some more pouches that could hang from her belt. She pushed away the feeling of homesickness that was already starting to form in her belly, and through her overwhelming flitting thoughts, she half-heartedly wondered if she would even get the chance to sup that night. Ready to leave, she hugged her mother goodbye, drank in the smell of the lilacs that wafted off her hair, and took time to savor the warm, comfortable feeling that would too soon be gone. Her myriad of emotions settled into hard determination, and she proudly replied to the knight now standing by her table: "You can tell the prince that my name is Aylan."

-o

Chapter 3
~ Royally Royalty ~

In many of the castle's cool rooms there hung gorgeous hand-woven tapestries. Some depicted scenes of nature, some of women in pretty dresses, some were of creatures like unicorns, which may or may not actually exist. One depicted a battle which showed Carn himself fighting some kind of beast with wings. The room this one hung in belonged to the prince, and had a vast fireplace in one wall which could give off heat in waves. On an adjacent wall there were a couple of windows near the corner. This was the prince's favourite spot, as it had a chair that was positioned in order to make it possible for him to both enjoy the view of his quarters and that of the courtyard, and allowed him to hear the sounds of the marketplace below. He had thick piled carpets of ruby-red, purple and gold in several places so his royal feet wouldn't get cold on the flagstone floor. In an inner chamber, the huge canopied bed was the centre of attention, with velvety drapes that hung down the sides to provide darkness and privacy for its occupant.

Things were peaceful right now with the sound of the birds that sung outside, yet the prince paced impatiently back and forth in his bedroom's lavish outer chamber.

"You're going to wear a path right down the centre of your rug," announced Carn, as he waited with the prince for Aylan's arrival. The prince gave him an exasperated look and took a seat on the cushioned armchair by the window, where he sat occasionally shifting around, exuding impatience.

"Why do girls always take so long to get ready? What do they *do* in their chambers?" complained the prince. "Just once I'd like to arrive on time for an occasion, but I spend half my time waiting for my three sisters to primp and preen and try on four dresses before they're ever satisfied! As well, after all that, they still always come out looking the same as when they went in! And now it seems that that is what it is like with *all* girls. What are they waiting for, a miracle to occur-?"

"Now, now," admonished Carn, cutting him off in the middle of his ranting. "Your sisters are not just any girls. They are three princesses who are going to be of marrying age in a few short months. They are expected to act and look like ladies. It is as much of a burden to them as clearing out the stalls is to the stable boy, or your sword fighting is to you when you tire of doing drills. We do what is expected of us because we must."

Just then, as they chatted in front of the prince's vast fireplace, the two heard an argument in full swing coming from the hall.

"Where *is* he?" a forceful female voice demanded.

"In the prince's chambers, but you mustn't go in there without being summoned, and especially not looking like this!" a woman argued, "It's not proper, it simply isn't done!"

The prince and Carn exchanged a worried look.

"It's only not done because no one has ever done it before!" the younger voice pointed out, and then amid shrieks and protests, the chamber doors burst open admitting two servants and a red-faced sopping wet Aylan, still fully clothed. She found Carn with her eyes, and let him have it. "Tell these women that I do *not* have to have a bath!" She stood, fists on her hips as a multitude of bubbles continued to pop on her head, and her clothes began to form quite a formidable puddle on the prince's intricate red carpet. Filled with indignation, she hurled at him: "I will be eleven years old in only three days and I know when and how to take my own baths!"

Carn looked pointedly at her wet clothes and replied in a good natured voice, "Oh come now, most of the people in this palace see it as a privilege and quite relaxing to have servants wait on them hand and foot. Besides, your ability to bathe yourself remains to be seen. I don't know how you do it on the farm, but folks around here usually disrobe to take their baths!" he chuckled.

Anger flashed inside Aylan, and hot tears of embarrassment sprung to her eyes, threatening to spill over her lower lids. This was a serious matter as far as she was concerned. She had been treated roughly, manhandled, and now instead of justice, she was being laughed at! She felt her short nails bite into her palms as her fingers curled into fists. She filled her lungs to give Carn another piece of her mind, but was interrupted as the men's attention was diverted across the room.

Bowing, one of the servants, a grey haired portly woman in a grey-brown frock and white apron interjected, "I'm afraid that was Millie's doing, Sir," she said humbly while keeping her eyes on the floor, "This girl saw the gown she was to wear and refused to give us her old clothes! She put up such a fight that I'm afraid Millie lost her temper and threw her into the bathwater, clothes and all!"

Stern faced, the prince stood up from his place by the window and approached Aylan, careful not to step in the growing puddle. "You enter my castle, disobey orders and insult my hospitality in my own home!" the prince scolded haughtily. "Why do you hate the dress that was picked out for you? It is one that used to be my sister's. It was one of her favourites.   You're very lucky to have an opportunity to wear it.   Is it not fine enough for you?"

"Because it's a *gown*!" she argued.

"And *you* are a *girl*!" he responded automatically.

"And no one ever accused *me* of being a *lady*!" She shot back.

"Maybe that's because you definitely don't act like one!   Perhaps with a little training-" he started, but never got a chance to finish, because at that moment, the soaked to the bone Aylan took her opportunity and seized the prince.   She moved in a flash.   Before anyone could stop her, she leapt toward the prince, enfolding his neck in the circle of one sopping arm, forcing him down.

"Maybe with a little training, you'd be able to get out of this headlock!" she retorted.

Instantly Carn was up, sword drawn, ready to act on any threat to the throne.

"Calm yourself, Carn", ordered the prince triumphantly from the girl's armpit, "*This* is my Aylan!   And I," he said to her, "am Prince Oslan, at your service."

-ȯ-

Chapter 4
~ A Second First Impression ~

Aylan nervously ran her fingertips along the soft velvety chair cushion she sat on while a servant poured her drink. She added cool milk and honey to her cup and stirred. The spoon clinked against the sides of the cup as steam rose lazily into the air, lifting the pleasant aroma to her nose. The serving girl finished pouring the drinks, and left Aylan and the prince to talk in peace.

Oslan, Aylan noticed now that they were seated across from each other, was built both strong and sturdy. He was also handsome, not that she'd ever admit it to anyone, even under the threat of torture. He had thick chestnut brown hair that was just starting to grow long enough for it to curl at the ends. He had a wide forehead, a strong jaw, and eyes that were a piercing colour a little too green to be hazel, that lit up his face.

She felt a brief flicker of a butterfly's wing in her tummy, and was secretly glad she had agreed to come. The prince was twelve years old, and seemed fair, although once he had come up with an idea, apparently he would not be swayed from it. To resolve the issue of Aylan and Millie's treatment of each other, he had had a new bath prepared for Aylan. She had been allowed to bathe and go about her grooming routine on her own. However, Millie was also declared Aylan's new hand maiden for the duration of her stay at the castle. She would be her personal servant; doing Aylan's mending, laying out her clothes, filling her pitcher and emptying her basin. Millie would also help her with her correspondence and be her companion. They would just have to learn to get along, Aylan realized with chagrin, or life in the castle was going to be made very, very hard.

"The reason I summoned you to tea is twofold," started the prince. "I was watching out my window and saw what you did to that thief in the marketplace. I believe I may be able to use you, if you wouldn't mind stepping up to the job that is. Not to mention that I find your manner highly entertaining!"

The sting of embarrassment heated her cheeks. "I'm glad I amuse you, your highness," she mumbled through gritted teeth. "In what way would you wish to use me?" she asked cautiously.

"I would like my father's mage, Lazelan, to train you to become my mage."

Aylan had begun sipping her drink, and at this point, the strong hot brew she had been drinking flew from her mouth, covering Oslan with a spray of fine mist. "Ahem," he cleared his throat while wiping off his face, "Though I admit that at some times I do find you more entertaining than at others."

"I'm so sorry, Your Highness!" Aylan sputtered. "You took me by surprise!"

"I apologize," he replied, "Remind me never to surprise you when you are eating something meaty with gravy that might stain!"

Aylan felt her cheeks blaze as she flushed a deep crimson red which warmed her face all the way up to her ears. Embarrassed, she changed the subject back to the one at hand. "But you don't need me, I only know how to throw a little dust around, I'm no mage. Mages work with real magic if there is such a thing. My fire dust is only herbs, science really. Besides," she added, "what could you want with me when you have Lazelan?"

"It is true that I have Lazelan's aid now, but his home is far away I fear, and he longs to return there. He came to us by accident years ago. He was sailing with a group of men on a trading expedition. Their plan was to trade for herbs, spices, livestock, and anything else that would prove useful. He is from a large town with a university, and was sent by his teacher to learn all he could and then pass on his knowledge to another. Once he had done that, he would be allowed to return home to start his own family and take a prestigious position at the university there. He explained to me that the process would take two to three years to finish his learning and prove himself as teacher to a student. Unfortunately, his ship never completed its journey.

The trading party had been anxious to leave as harvest time was upon them. They didn't want to miss the chance to buy something that they may be able to use and they didn't want their tradable goods to spoil. They had been warned by a seer that if they left within the fortnight, that disaster would befall them. They had scoffed at the idea as they were travelling with seasoned sailors who would know what to do in any situation. Besides, they did not put much credence in the ability of seers who claimed to see the future, a mistake they may have learned to correct, if still alive today. The boat launched two days later, but while most of them had felt nothing but ease, Lazelan had felt unease. They had sailed about half way, and had begun to notice the swells of waves growing larger when the mighty storm hit.

It was dawn, the sun should have been rising, but the sky remained dark, the air filled with mist. The cloud cover was so deep and murky that it seemed almost sinister, as if it had been sent there to mock them. Now the sailors were beginning to feel jittery. Lighting began hitting tall trees on far-off shorelines, and it was the only light they had to see by. The air was filled with the scent of electricity as thunder boomed across the sky, rolling out in waves like the waters below. The salt-smelling sea became rougher still. The waves swelled and rolled until they started to crash upon the deck itself, washing away goods, supplies and men alike. Everyone was drenched to the bone from the mingling freezing cold waves and thick fog. The calls of "Man overboard!" were hard to hear as the crack of the thunder echoed through the sky. Then, as the boat was tossed about like a young child's toy, keening to one side, lightning hit the mainsail's mast. The sail burst into flames which were half extinguished by the rain that began to drive down, pelting the boat and sailors with cold spears of water. This continued until his boat was dashed apart on invisible rocks that destroyed it in the clash of the storm.

A few men who could swim and many more that could not, were lost to the sea. Others drifted to one place or another on pieces of the ship's debris, and still others were simply never to be heard from again. Lazelan was one of the lucky ones that had been able to swim. He swam for hours, and when he was too cold and tired to move any further, he simply floated there, looking up at the sky. He eventually floated near enough to shore that he was spotted by some of our kingdom's fishermen. They hauled him aboard and brought him back to safety. Being unconscious and dressed in strange clothing, he was brought before the guards of the castle for interrogation.

He told the guards his story, and they brought him before my father, great King Eurilas, who did not believe in magic. The teenager must have done something impressive indeed to convince him, because when he left the room, not only was my father convinced of the existence of magic, but he had offered the boy a job at his right hand. My father sent a messenger to Lazelan's university explaining what had happened, and asked that Lazelan be allowed to stay and work for a while without jeopardizing his place at the university. The professor and Lazelan's family agreed as long as he still performed the duties they had sent him away for, and so he has stayed with us. It has been a long while, and he misses them very much. He had been courting a maid there and woos her still through lengthy love letters. He now wishes to seek out the woman that has waited these long years for him to marry her. His fortune is now grand enough that they shall want for nothing. However, though he has learned and become a more promising mage, he has yet to train an apprentice before he may return to start his family.

I was only eight when he joined us, so I have grown up these last years with Lazelan, and I too believe in the existence of magic. I have come to also believe that every good king should have a mage on his side. I am the heir to the throne and in a few short years I will need someone I can trust, someone who will work with me to make this a fine place to live for all of the kingdom's subjects. I have seen you in action. I know your heart is pure and your actions are just. You have been one of this kingdom's subjects and have worked her land, so I know you can give me a fresh perspective on what my people might need. Besides...," he waited for her to swallow and added with a gleam in his eye, "I can't ascend to the throne until I have taken a wife."

Chapter 5
~ Acceptance ~

Aylan carefully set down her teacup and saucer as they began to noticeably clink together. "Your highness," she began, now blushing to the roots of her hair. "I am not yet eleven, and marrying age is thirteen! Are you...are you...*proposing?*"

Oslan let out a gale of deep laughter and replied, "I see you have the same aversion to marriage at this point as I. No, no, fear not the life sentence, the old ball and chain. I only meant that if you will join me and work with Lazelan," he continued in a conspiratorial whisper, "I have a plan!"

Aylan sat quietly and thought a while. *This is the chance of a lifetime! I suddenly have the prospects of a bright future instead of being stuck as a farmer for the rest of my life. And to be able to learn more herbology...maybe even learn if there really is such a thing as real magic!* Finally she said: "But I know all the herbology that is possible with the plants that grow in this area, Highness. What could he possibly teach me here at the castle that I haven't already learned in the fields? And even if there were things to learn and I came to stay here, then what about Mother? She cannot run the farm all by herself. I have a duty to her, and I would miss her so much."

"Oh, I think you will find that there are many, many things yet to learn. The king's forest is a rich store for herbs and plants the likes of which have never seen. Also, Lazelan would be spending more of his time teaching you actual magic. I believe some call it magic of the mind to distinguish it from herbology and cheap parlor tricks. As for your mother, the castle would provide one of our servants for her to take your place, of course," Oslan assured her. "You would both have the freedom to visit each other every weekend. You would not be a prisoner Aylan, only a student...and perhaps my friend."

Excitement flooded her, and once again that butterfly wing fluttered in her tummy. *Then magic does exist!* She thought, feeling as though she had stumbled onto a great secret. "Then I see no reason not to, Your Highness," she said simply.

"Excellent!" he crooned. "From this moment on, let me be only *Your Highness* in front of the court. Now, I am just Oslan to you, my little mage," he informed her. "I'm afraid there is something that you're not going to like though," he continued.

"Oh? What's that?" she asked.

"I'm afraid you *are* going to have to wear a gown as befits a lady, when I present you to the court as my mage!" he instructed.

"When I am fully a mage, I shall worry about it then!" she managed through gritted teeth.

*   *   *

Aylan returned to her room to mull things over, whereupon she received a shock as she found Millie going through her things. Her newly appointed hand maiden had thick wavy black locks just past her shoulders and deep brown eyes, which were presently staring intently at Aylan's few belongings. Aylan eyed the girl suspiciously and watched to see what she would do. Millie wore the standard castle servants' livery, which consisted of a grayish-brown skirt, black bodice and white shirt and apron. She was slightly plump and short for her age, putting them at odds. She was also thirteen, almost two full years older than Aylan. This was a fact Millie never failed to remind Aylan of, though the two girls were about the same height. Aylan could hear her various vials clink together as Millie's plump fingers rummaged around in the satchel of herbs. She had found Aylan's soft yellow pouch of dust and had some pinched between her fingers, feeling it. Panicked, and realizing this had gone too far, Aylan jumped into action.

"Whatever you do, don't drop that!" Aylan warned urgently. Millie froze in place, shoulders tensed. Without moving, she answered, "I won't, why not?"

Aylan approached her carefully, and taking the bag from her, she pulled the drawstring closed and attached it to her belt. She then gently took Millie's wrist and led her over to her jug of water and wash basin. She held Millie's citrusy-smelling dust covered fingers over the basin and filled it up. Together, they lowered Millie's hand into the cool water. Once the last piece of dust was submerged, Aylan told her: "Ok, that should do it. The water neutralizes the fire and burning potential of the dust. You can wash your hand like normal now without any danger." Then she added quietly, "I would like to talk to you about why you were going through my things when you're done."

Five minutes later, Aylan and Millie were sitting across from each other in the small room. Letting the silence pan out between them, Aylan surveyed her surroundings as she waited for Millie's answer. The hand maid sat on one of the two wooden stools, while Aylan had chosen a spot on her bed where she could face the other girl. The room was rectangular, with only one thin rug on the floor. Aside from the bed, her chest of things and stools, there was a writing desk, and wash basin for washing her hands and face. There were five hooks on the wall provided to hang garments, but the only one there was the dreaded crystal blue ball gown of Oslan's sister, Tanyan. They were on the third floor of the keep, and had two doorways in the room, one to enter by, and a second that led to a balcony that overlooked the garden. Millie's crumpled bed lay against one wall.

Millie sat for a while just thinking, and flashes of guilt flitted across her face, only to be replaced by a look of pure defiance. Finally, she spoke up, "I wanted to know what made *you* so special!" she announced. "You're no better than I, you grew up on a farm, and I grew up in this castle! You don't know how to act as a noble woman, yet I have studied them all my life! And yet he picks you out of everyone in the kingdom and offers to give you everything, while I have been around him and his genteel friends since they were born, and yet I am invisible."

"Maybe I'm not the first one you've thrown into a bath fully clothed?" Aylan said pointedly. "I'm pretty sure you got his attention with that stunt today."

"It's not *his* attention I long for," sighed Millie, blushing faintly as she looked down at her hands in her lap.

"Regardless, if you wanted to know more about me, you should have just asked. I happen to know a little about magic, and that is what the prince is interested in. I'm not here to change who I am, I like living on the farm, though it's not as extravagant as this. My aunt happens to be the Countess of Eshenberg, so I do know how to act as a lady. But this," she explained while motioning to her tunic and hose, "is who I am, not some dolled up little girl to be waited upon. I enjoy the freedom to do things for myself."

At the mention of magic, Millie's head jerked up as she forgot all about averting her eyes as a servant should, and when Aylan mentioned her relation to the well-known countess, her hand maid's eyes widened. "I stand corrected, Milady. You are the better woman."

Aylan surprised her by laughing. "I'm hardly yet a woman; I won't be of marrying age for over a year! Besides, I'm no better Millie, just different. You know a lot about things that I don't, like how the ladies at court like to wear their hair, or the latest fashions, and I know about other things, like how to hogtie a pig, or magic.

At this, Millie began to warm up to her mistress. It was becoming obvious to Millie that Aylan truly was not like the other girls of the court, with their noses so stuck up they sometimes seemed as if they could get lost in the clouds. She appreciated that for once she was working for someone that actually saw her as a person, not just as a servant that was meant to be used and seen but not heard. She relaxed a little. "I'm sorry," she ventured, "for overstepping my bounds with you once again. I give you my word that it won't happen again."

"I appreciate that," she assured Millie. "I believe I should teach you how to properly handle my things, in case I need you to fetch them for me. I don't want to scare you, but had you dropped my pouch and had it landed open, you could have set us and everything in this room on fire."

Millie's mouth went dry. "I'm sorry", she whispered. "I didn't realize, I didn't know-"

"I know, I know", Aylan soothed, "but it is knowledge you should have. This is the easy stuff, herbology, but had I used real magic to I don't know...put a hex on my things, goodness knows what might have happened to you for touching them."

"What do you mean herbology, real magic?"

"There are two ways in which magic exists". Aylan explained. "Herbology is what I use in my pouches and vials. I know that certain plants have certain properties; juices and fibres that they are made of and things that they can do. For example, when your tummy is upset, making a tea out of a plant called ginger will soothe and calm it. Some of these plants can be mixed to do extraordinary things, some are used independently. But mixing them, or using them the wrong way can be very dangerous."

"You would teach me these things?" Millie enquired.

"I will teach you what you must know to keep you safe, and more if you would like to learn." Aylan agreed. "Can you read?"

"Yes!" Millie said proudly. "My father said that one must be at one's best to fully serve in the castle. He knows what I know; that servants aren't stupid people. He taught us to read at a young age because it is useful. I used to hate practicing my letters, but he used to say: "But what if a noble asks you to fetch something with a label that you cannot read?" Millie boasted in her best imitation of her father's voice. Then her countenance changed and she became somber again. "But, Milady, you said that there are two types of magic. What is the second?"

"The other is more clandestine, and I honestly didn't know it really existed for sure until today. It is called "magic of the mind", and it encompasses a child's concept of magic. Simply put, you use your mind and incantations to make things turn into reality. This is what I am to learn here at the castle, starting tomorrow.   But as I said, it is a secret thing, so you mustn't tell a soul about it."

"Oh, I shan't!" promised Millie, but Aylan still wondered if she could truly be trusted.

Chapter 6
~ Skirdkhen ~

Oslan had come to Aylan's chamber to fetch her first thing after breakfast the next day, donning a sword that looked far too big for the boy. Aylan eyed it doubtfully as she got ready, collecting various pouches of herbs and vials of pastes and liquids. "What are you going to do while I'm studying for the day?" she asked.

"I will be studying too," he replied, "today I train with Carn and Ormond. They teach me attacks and defenses, footing, and how to outsmart an opponent that fights dirty."

"You actually fight with that thing?" she asked, motioning to his giant sword. "Isn't it heavy? Aren't you afraid that you'll get hurt?" Aylan's questions tumbled out one after another.

As they started down the hall together, footfalls echoing off the stone walls, the prince answered her as best he could. "Yes my sword is heavy, but not as heavy as the next will be. We train with swords of different weights, lengths and even swords made out of different things. When we start, we use wooden swords, then swords made out of heavier wood. We move onto metal swords, and the swords get bigger and heavier as our muscles and skills grow. The only difficult part is changing over to a new sword. You have to adjust your skills and get used to the new feel and weight of it." He explained. Then he motioned down a corridor off to their left. "A quick detour if you wouldn't mind, I would like to show you something special."

Oslan turned down the hall, where Aylan could see two guards standing against one wall. When they caught sight of the prince, they seemed to straighten perceptively. As Oslan and Aylan approached, she realized that the guards were actually standing on either side of a set of heavy wooden double doors. They both made a gesture of laying their gauntlet-clad right hands over their breastplates. While the sound of their armour still rang in the air, the prince's cloth garments rustled as he mimicked the movement and the guards moved to allow him entrance. They passed through the open door to a room that smelled of metal, wood, and oiled leather. "What was that?" Aylan asked, copying the movement.

"That is our salute," he explained, "It is used by anyone in the king's service. It means that they serve with their hearts. It is a signal that they are here by choice, because they love the king and are ready to follow him wholeheartedly. They salute me as a brother fighter, and acknowledge that they too are here to serve me. I signal them back to show my appreciation and tell them that I too would protect them. The lords and ladies of the court have also adopted a similar motion. You may have seen it. They have taken our salute one step further. It is now common to see young or old, people in love will lay their hand over their heart and extend it to the other person palm up," he showed her as he spoke, "to tell their partners that they love them with their whole heart and that their heart belongs only to them."

They had stopped in front of a wall adorned with pieces of armor, shields and weapons. On the far wall was a door, and aside from that, the room was filled with implements of battle. "This is the armory," explained the prince. The wall they were facing had a huge sword as a focal centerpiece. It was laid upon a beautifully carved wooden rack all on its own. The hilt was jet black and gold. Beautiful etchings of the same dragon head that appeared on Carn's armour were inlaid into both sides, and the thick blade carried another dragon breathing fire down its length. The blade's edge was wavy, and although one edge was smooth and looked razor sharp, the other was serrated, and etched like the scales on a dragon's back.

"It's magnificent", she breathed in awe.

"It is called Skirdkhen, and it belonged to Jonnohlenn the Gentle."

"The *Gentle?*" she asked incredulously, "Someone with the title of gentle wielded *that?*"

The prince nodded solemnly "He was a mighty king. He ruled for almost sixty years. That's almost unheard of, you know. Most kings' reigns only last for anywhere between three to thirty years tops, but he created a peaceful kingdom. It is said that there was only one battle after he took the throne. It was when he was an old man. He had had Skirdkhen made for him for his coronation and swore that he would never need it while he reigned. He was as good as his word, and it hung above his throne in the throne room as a symbol of peace. He had had only daughters, and they too, so one of the nephews would be the next to take on the throne.

One day, when he was an old man, two of Jonnohlenn's younger nephews came to bow before him one day and beseech him to stop their brother, Gorin. They came in front of the court to warn the king that their older brother was a greedy sort, and was even now plotting to take troops into the neighbouring kingdom to acquire more land without seeking the king's approval or his permission. Astonished at the bold move, Jonnohlenn thought fast, calling for his general to discuss strategy. He knew that if Gorin's small army of underlings were to go marching in on the next kingdom, their ruler would see it as a sign of war. He commanded the general to take a small contingent of troops to head Gorin's group off before they reached his kingdom's boarder, but the order turned out to be unnecessary. The murmurs of the courtiers were hushed as Gorin appeared in the throne room doorway, over six feet tall and in full battle armor. He strode down the red isle runner toward the king. The sound of metal striking metal resounded through the hall as he approached. He eyed his brothers as he passed, hand on his sword, saying "I'll deal with you lot later." Their breaths caught sharply in their throats at the sound of his ragged voice, and they began to stink of fear. Gorin stopped in front of the king's throne, but neglected to bow, this was a challenge to the king.

"Bow before your king, you insolent fool!" raged the general, his hand going to the hilt of his sword.

"I don't recall choosing him as *my* king." Gorin replied, "This kingdom needs a king that is willing to fortify his country by expanding its borders, strengthening its army in case of attack, and should let courtiers live as they please! Perhaps you should step down and let someone take the throne that is willing to make this country great, someone like me!"

All those present gasped at the tirade. It was against the law to openly speak out against the throne's policy. Any change was brought about in meetings with the king in private. What's more, refusing to bow before the king was an offence akin to treason and was punishable by death. If that hadn't been enough, his last angry words doubted the king's ability to lead, it was a verbal attack against the throne, and meant death on the spot.

The general pulled out his sword and went for Gorin, but Gorin was faster. He drew his weapon and took the general down, right at the foot of the throne's stairs. The king stood, shaking his head sadly. "This is inexcusable, Gorin, I will not have you murdering people! I thought maybe I could talk some reason into you. We do not need to fortify our armies; we have been a peaceful nation for sixty years! We have everything we need on the land we already own, so we do not need to extend our borders. And lastly, I will not have slavery in my kingdom. I abolished that forty years ago, and if nobles are still unhappy about it, they can go to live in a place that allows that kind of barbaric lifestyle! I will not allow you to march on another kingdom and end my reign of peace!"

Gorin started mounting the stairs toward the king and his wife. Weapon still drawn, he grabbed for the queen and growled: "If you will not raise a sword for your kingdom, perhaps we do need fresh blood on the throne!" He clutched the small queen's head to his chest, bringing his sword up toward her throat. The king turned with a grace and agility that was much younger than his seventy years. He reached for Skirdkhen, unsheathing it as he turned. He completed his swivel, slicing through the air above his wife's head. There was a flash and the smell of sulphur, and Gorin's body fell limply to the ground.

After that, Jonnohlenn descended the stairs, taking his wife's arm to steady her. He approached his two remaining nephews and spoke to the oldest in front of the court. "Cemtnyracc, you will have the throne now. I swore I would never use Skirdkhen while I ruled, needing it was a sign, and so I shall now pass the throne on to you. Use my laws as guidance and you shall enjoy a long and peaceful reign as I have enjoyed."

Everyone in the court stood dumbfounded as

the king and queen peacefully left the throne room as if his rein were not at an end. Cemtnyracc ascended to the throne platform, and looking down at the body of Gorin, he saw a remarkable thing: Skirdkhen had not only beheaded his brother, but had left mysterious scorch marks on the skin, as if from the breath of a dragon's fire."

Chapter 7
~ Child Prodigy ~

"She is about to arrive," said a pretty female voice from behind the door. "She will enter in approximately fifty-three seconds, once the prince convinces her to. She waits behind the door now."

Aylan paused at the sound of the voice as she reached for the doorknob. She let her arm drop. She and the prince were currently standing in a stone hallway in the second level of the castle. Aylan had learned that morning that the castle had more to offer than what originally met the eye. From the armoury, Oslan had taken her into the war room through the door opposite from where the guards stood. The war room was rectangular and had a huge heavy wooden table taking up most of the room. Rudimentary maps lay on the table, and heavy chairs were positioned around it. Taking up a whole wall, floor to ceiling and almost corner to corner was another tapestry. This one depicted the whole kingdom including the castle, farms, forests, roads and rivers. She stared at it for a long time, noticing that each lord's manor was signified by his family coat of arms. The prince motioned her closer to him, and when she approached he pointed at a group of pastures and cropland. "This is your house", he told her. She looked closer, smelling the dust in the old tapestry, astonished that her little family had been represented. Before she could comment on it, the prince seized the edge of the tapestry and disappeared behind it. His hand appeared at the edge of it and waited. She stepped forward and took the hand before her. He pulled her into a hidden space in the wall, and into a secret passage that lay behind the gigantic tapestry of the king's lands. They followed the musty narrow passageway to a staircase. They mounted the stairs and continued on until they came to the door before which they now stood.

"Go ahead," urged the prince, "they are expecting us."

"But what is this place?" she enquired.

"This is Lazelan's well hidden workroom. This is where you will spend some of your time training every day. I have entrusted you with this secret location, Aylan, I hope you can appreciate how important it is that this place remain non-existent to the outside world. Not even the general nor his soldiers that use the war room know that it is here."

"I can be trusted Oslan, but I have a feeling that you already know that, otherwise you wouldn't have brought me here." The prince nodded at her assumption. "But the question I have, Prince, is why do I hear a girl's voice? I know you said Lazelan was a boy. Was that just a story that is part of keeping the truth a secret?"

The prince chuckled. "No Aylan, the story I told you about Lazelan is true. But there are secrets just as precious as the whereabouts of this room, one of which is on the other side of this door." At this the prince reached past her and lifted the latch. The first cracks of candle light were visible as she heard a handsome voice say: "Ah, right as always!"

A ringing laughter, then the door swung open enough to reveal Lazelan and the owner of the pretty female voice that was talking once again.

"But of course, Silly, I wouldn't be much good if there was a chance I could be wrong!"

"Sasha," Lazelan pressed, "How many times do I have to tell you that there is nothing silly about me?"

"Ah, Lazelan," she mused, "always the

serious type. Lighten up a little, you just might have some fun! And what have you brought us, Oslan, another serious one?" she asked, turning to the prince.

"Sasha, I have brought you your fun personified." Oslan told her as he put his warm hand on the small of Aylan's back and urged her forward. "Sasha, Lazelan, this is Aylan, our new mage in training, your new protégé. Aylan, meet Lazelan, your new teacher."

"You mean-" Lazelan jumped up and took the prince's hand, shaking it.

"Yes my friend, you will shortly be able to return home to your Magdolyn. And I hope I will be invited to the wedding, of course!" he winked.

"Maggie will be so pleased! There wouldn't be a wedding without you being there!" he assured.

"Well technically," pointed out Aylan, "As long as you two and the officiant show up it's a done deal."

Everyone paused and looked at Aylan. Then all three burst out laughing as Aylan felt heat rise to her cheeks while she blushed. "What did I tell you Lazelan?" the prince said, "Maybe she will be able to teach you to lighten up," he teased.

Sasha stood and cleared her throat. When she stood, Aylan could see how very tall she was. She was almost the same height as Lazelan, who was a head and a half taller than Aylan herself. She was graceful and seemed to carry herself like a noble. She wore a dress of gold, with gold rope trim, and had long flowing golden hair of almost the same shade as her dress. Her eyes were light brown, and her skin was cream coloured without a freckle in sight. Aylan's first instinct was to be jealous, but the girl seemed so genuinely nice that Aylan found she couldn't think a bad thought about her. She approached Aylan and kissed her quickly on both cheeks. "We will be as sisters one day," she confided in a low sweet voice, "Till then, I look forward to being your friend." Aylan found she liked this girl already and felt that they were already old friends though they had just met. She stood there not really knowing what to say.

"She has that effect on people", the prince remarked, "But I am being rude, Aylan, this is Sasha, our seer."

"Seer?" Aylan gawked.

"A real child prodigy," insisted Lazelan, "At the young age of two and a half, she saved her entire village when she had nightmares foretelling a fire that was to take the whole community. Her family was used to her dreams coming true in an eerie way by this point, so they told people to start conserving the rain in their rain barrels. Those that knew of her dreams coming true dampened their thatched roofs and were extra careful of their hearth fires. Then one night soon after Sasha's dream, it happened. A fire at someone's hearth threw a spark onto a woven mat. The man that lived there had fallen asleep in a chair by the fire, and couldn't stop a flame from erupting in time. Luckily, the houses around that one were thoroughly wetted down, and people had enough water on hand to put out the fire before it spread to the other nearby domiciles. The village was saved."

"She," the prince nodded at Sasha, "Is our other best kept secret."

-o-
-◇-

Chapter 8
~ A Mysterious Odour ~

"Ugh!" complained Sasha the next day, "What are you two doing, making perfume for an orc? That stuff smells like a skunk! Seriously, the odour is so bad that I think my *vision* is being blurred!"

"Stop being so melodramatic Sasha," Lazelan chided in a hushed voice, "Aylan has been working very hard, and she's doing quite well. In fact," he added, looking over at Aylan's concoction, "Just a little more lizard root and I think she's got it!"

Across the workroom, Aylan sat with her eyes near the rim of the bowl that was holding her newest attempt at magic. She sniffed her creation and wrinkled her nose in disgust. She looked around at the various vials and pouches set around her. She selected a pouch, and withdrew a couple of things that looked like very small lizard shaped yellow twigs. With just the tip of her tongue poking out between her lips in concentration, she looked very studious as she dropped two tiny bits of the root into the bowl to see what would happen. She grabbed a pestle and ground up the bits into the paste. The mixture began to lighten slightly and the odour became even more pungent. Lazelan crowed excitedly. He came over to where Aylan was working and clapped her on the shoulder.

"Well done, well done indeed!" he exclaimed. How did you know to add more lizard root?"

"The smell was wrong. It seemed like that was what was missing." Aylan hedged.

"Listen to that!" Lazelan boasted to Sasha, "She is not only following instructions, but the girl can problem solve too! Aylan, I was excited when Oslan found me a student, but I am truly proud to be your teacher. You are a natural at this. Most students wouldn't think to use their noses. With most it is only what they can see with their eyes or read in a book. You experiment, try new things and use all of your senses to gain the information you need! Very impressive," Aylan beamed, filled with a sense of pride at Lazelan's excitement over her work.

Sasha came over and peered into the bowl. "Yep, that's what I saw. Now all you need to do is roll it into balls."

Lazelan's jaw dropped and he stared at Sasha. "How do *you* know that? I haven't even told Aylan what this potion is for yet."

Sasha replied: "Oh have some faith Lazelan, I dreamed this whole thing last night. I even saw you rejoice! It was really nice to have a dream where happiness was the focus for a change. I knew Aylan would get this right before she even picked up her first ingredient."

Aylan looked at her astonished. "You mean you could see what ingredients I used and everything? What is stopping you from becoming a mage too then?"

Sasha grinned. "Too much work," she joked. "Seriously though, I could see what you were reaching for, and your reaction to adding each thing, but not necessarily how much of each thing you were adding, or what was inside the pouches you reached for. I could see your joy, Lazelan's, and the end result, but that's about it. I didn't see enough to know how to make it myself, just that you would be successful."

Aylan looked at Lazelan, puzzled. "So now I have to roll this paste into balls? To what purpose?"

Lazelan instructed the girl to take a bit of thick paste between her first finger and thumb. He showed her how to roll it around until it was basically round.   Aylan copied his actions swiftly, making an almost perfect sphere.   "Aylan, you have just made your first pill."   Lazelan said, setting his aside to dry further.

"You mean I have to put that awful smelling stuff in my mouth?"

"And you have to swallow!" chimed in Sasha gleefully.

"Ew, oh no Lazelan! Aylan cried in revulsion, "There has got to be a limit here somewhere, if I eat that I'll be sick! There is nothing that could make me want to consume that."

"Pinch your nose, you might not taste it...much!" offered Sasha.

"You don't have to eat it if you don't want Aylan," Lazelan told her, "But what the pills do just might be worth the bad taste."

"Well what do they do?" demanded Aylan as she rolled more paste into balls.

"Ah, but that would be cheating if I told you. You will remember much more easily if you experience it for yourself."

Aylan looked at Sasha pointedly.   "Do you know what they do?"

"I have a pretty good idea." She replied, looking at Lazelan with an intrigued expression.

"This is so frustrating!" Aylan fumed as she finished rolling the last of the brown paste. Lazelan told her to leave the balls there to dry, and that they would work on something new after lunch. He sent her out to go wash up and told her that he and Sasha would catch up with her when the food was ready. Aylan put away all of her things on a shelf that Lazelan had set aside for her potions.   She opened the door and breathed deeply, tasting the fresh air outside the tiny room and left to prepare for the meal.

"I really am quite amazed" Lazelan confided in Sasha. "I have never seen a student as young as Aylan take on a recipe of this calibre with such efficiency. She will be an amazing herbologist. I would even venture to say that she is one already.

"That's nothing," Sasha replied, "I haven't told you yet the rest of my dream. Aylan will do real magic."

"That is not hard to believe," said Lazelan, "The girl shows much promise, in as soon as a year she may be ready, much sooner than I had hoped. It won't be long before I will have to start teaching her the Almatrae alphabet so she can begin to study spells."

"Oh it will be much sooner than that," Sasha confessed, "But I'm afraid you won't be there to coach her through her first time." She added.

"But of course I will, no one can use it untrained, that part of your brain lies dormant until you have been instructed how to open your mind to use it. It is almost unheard of to tap into that source without months of instruction."

"And perhaps," Sasha ventured, "It would be completely unheard of, to have it happen while you sleep?"

-ȯ

-ọ-

Chapter 9
~ Just Gone ~

After an exhausting afternoon of mixing ingredients over a hot flame, Aylan returned to her room once more to wash up and change for dinner. Millie was already there and had her clothes picked out and ready to go. At Aylan's request, the prince had provided her with a couple more tunics and hose like the ones she was already partial to in lieu of dressing gowns. By now, those that dined with her were used to seeing her in this kind of outfit and to her relief, had gotten over their aversion to seeing a girl in boy's clothes.

Millie had picked out her mistress' favourite tunic, the one she had been wearing the day Carn had found her at her cottage and had changed her life forever. It lay now on her bed beside a fresh pair of hose. Mille sat cross legged on her own mattress against the wall. She was currently sewing one of the sleeves of another of Aylan's shirts. Aylan had sprouted a lot in the past few weeks at the castle, and found that several of her shirts and hose were becoming too small. Rather than spend more money on new outfits when she was still quickly growing, Millie suggested that she take down the sleeves to get a bit more wear out of them.

Aylan entered the room and placed her new pills and the light blue potion she had made this afternoon with her notebook. She moved to the bed and flopped down beside her clean clothes, exhausted. After dinner, she would sit and write about the effects of the things she had made. She would also write down how she had made them, and tricks she had used that would make working with certain ingredients easier in the future. For now though, she just wanted to rest.

"Milady!" Millie protested, "You must get up and bathe!"

"Oh, not this again," Aylan groaned, "Don't you remember that I'm to be able to choose if and when I bathe myself!"

"Um, Milady?" Millie asked softly, "You are right, you are in charge of such things, it's just that well...pardon me for saying so, but you smell like a muddy yak."

Aylan groaned again from her place on her blanket. "It can't possibly be that bad, honestly." But when she looked up at Millie, she saw the girl was almost green in the face. She pulled the front of the tunic she was currently wearing up to her face to sniff the fabric, and started choking a little at the fumes wafting off of it. Her eyes began to water at the horrible smell, and groaning again, she climbed off her bed and headed for the wash basin to wash her hands and face.

"Do you want me to order you a bath, Milady?" Millie asked hopefully.

"I guess you'd better," Aylan sighed. "Can you take my clothes down to the laundry as well, please? I'm not sure that we would be able to sleep well tonight with this smell present."

"Yes, Milady," Millie responded, and took the clothes that Aylan handed her, taking special care not to gag audibly while still in the room with her mistress. She left to order the bath, telling Aylan that the tub would be up shortly.

Aylan finished washing her face and hands in her basin, and stood in the middle of the room contemplating her work from the afternoon. She approached her desk where the pills and new little vial lay, and picked up the tiny pouch. She extracted one of the pills and let it roll around in the palm of her hand. She sniffed it and pulled her head sharply back from the strong smell. It was about the size of her pinky fingernail, and looked to be a deep chocolate brown colour that was the consistency of dirt. She decided it would be better to get this over with now so she would not have to touch them again once clean. She closed her eyes, plugged her nose with the first finger and thumb of her left hand, and let the little pill fall into her mouth. She swallowed. Nothing happened. The pill remained in her mouth. Panicked, she raced to the wash basin and reached for the jug of clean water. She had to use both hands to lift its weight. No sooner had she let go of her nose, than the pungent smell of the pill lay down as a thick taste on her tongue. She gagged and hefted the jug, drinking directly from it in order to get the pill down as quickly as possible. Once the pill was swallowed, and Aylan had taken a few extra swigs of the water for good measure, she replaced the pitcher on its counter. The water hadn't completely washed away all of the taste that lingered in her mouth. *Millie was right*, she thought sickly, *my mouth tastes as if I just licked a muddy yak*. She contemplated the bar of soap, wondering if it would make her mouth taste any better, when she was interrupted in mid thought.

She spun at the sound of two men entering her room as they hefted the heavy wash tub inside. She froze, in the middle of her room wearing just her under-things. Millie had taken her clothes away to be washed, and Aylan had not yet grabbed a towel. One of the men poked his head in, peered around, and then proceeded to throw open the door while they both carried in the tub. They positioned it in the middle of the floor and stood for a moment mopping their brows.

"You'd think they wouldn't call for a tub unless they actually need one!" the first one complained.

"Maybe the little miss will be returning soon and the wench is just preparing so that things are ready for her."

"That's if the girl even bathes! I heard she was so against a bath when she arrived that a servant even had to throw her in clothes and all! I tell you, I would love to be able to bathe whenever I wanted! This girl doesn't know how good she's got it. And with hot water even!"

"She'll be mighty surprised if she arrives to a cold bath because it was ready too far in advance."

"Then the girl will probably decide never to bathe!" the men chortled meanly.

At this, Aylan, who had stood silently listening to every word while anger and astonishment at their gall rose inside her, picked up the first thing she could grab and tossed it at the two men full force. Sadly, the first thing that had been within grabbing distance at the time was her own wash basin that she had previously been washing her hands and face over. It flew across the room and smashed on the wall, just missing one of the men, but showering them both with dirty soapy water. They both screamed high-pitched womanly screams, and darted out the door yelling at the top of their lungs about the room being haunted.

Millie returned shortly after, to see the mess of pieces of broken clay on the floor. A towel also lay on the floor, soaking up the water that had been inside the broken basin. "Ah me, did the men speak the truth? Aylan?" she called as she searched the tiny room to find her mistress. "But where has she gone now, and without her clothes?" she asked herself as she looked at the tunic that still lay on the bed.

"Millie, I'm right here!" Aylan replied from where she knelt beside the mess on the floor. She started mopping up the water by moving around the towel.

Millie's head whipped around toward the sound and her eyes grew wide. "Milady? But where are you?"

"I'm right here!" Aylan replied impatiently, waving her hand in the air at her hand maid.

"Where?" asked Millie. "I can hear your voice, but I see you not!"

Aylan got up and walked over to Millie, who was looking around confused. "I am right in front of you!" she said, now growing impatient. "Stop playing these games, Millie. When is the water coming? I'm getting quite cold!"

Millie blinked in her direction and reached out with her hand. It bumped into something in front of her.

"Ouch, Millie, watch it, that was my chin!" Aylan exclaimed.

Millie gently reached out her hand again finding her mistress' face. "By the shields of the army of Ormond," she breathed, "Aylan, give me your hand, I'm afraid I have something to show you."

Aylan took Millie's hand and allowed her to lead her to the bed. "Sit right here now, and don't move!" Millie raced out of the room, leaving the door opened, and returned quickly with a mirror in hand.

"Millie, what am I going to do with you?" Aylan yelled, incensed. I am sitting here on my bed in nothing but my under garments, and you left the door wide open for all the world to see!"

"You need not have worried, mistress, look!"

Millie replied excitedly as she thrust a hand mirror in the direction of the indentation on the bed. Aylan stared, astonished as the wall behind her was reflected back in the mirror, and nothing else.

"Oh, Milady," Millie blurted out, "you've turned invisible!"

Chapter 10
~ A Match Made in Heaven ~

A short while later, after the bath was filled with piping hot water and the two girls knew they would be left without interruption, Aylan told Millie about the pills she had created that afternoon.

"Ugh! You can't really mean that you put one of those awful smelling things into your mouth!" Millie protested as Aylan showed her the pills that had made her invisible.

"I won't lie, the thing did taste vile, but don't you think it's worth it?" Aylan asked, excited. "I could go anywhere, do anything, and no one would be the wiser. Think of the implications of this Millie! If we made a whole slew of these, Ormond could take soldiers behind enemy lines in a war to rescue some of our men without even being seen!"

"It may not work as well as you are imagining, Milady. It is true that you can't be seen, but my other senses aren't fooled. Think of all the noise the king's men make in their clanging armour. And no offence, but you still smell like a yak! And who knows what other properties the pills have. Perhaps if they had to cross a river, the spell would be at an end and they would be seen once again. What is the duration or limits of the pills? I have a feeling any soldier still might be found out." Millie countered.

At the mention of Aylan still giving off an offensive odour, she walked to the desk, collected a light purple vial and poured some of its contents into the bath. The aroma of lilacs filled the air as the steam carried some of the scent out of the hot water. Aylan breathed deeply and thought fondly of home as she replaced the vial, and crossed back to the tub and began to climb in. "Let's test that theory, shall we?" As her feet and legs felt the soothing heat of the deep bath, she could see that they displaced the water, yet remained invisible. "Intriguing," she mumbled to herself as she sat down. The water pooled around her where she sat, so it seemed to have a big Aylan-shaped hole in it. Though she was still invisible, the water was obviously being pushed aside by something that was taking up space. "Well," she added, "this might be obvious to an observing eye."

"Or if not obvious," replied Millie, "still more than a tad unnatural. I think it might draw unwanted attention."

"Check. So avoid the water." Aylan agreed. "I suppose being out in the rain would create a similar problem. I propose that we test the limitations of this pill until dinnertime. We still have a couple of hours, you take one too, and we'll see what we can do."

"But we don't know how long the pills will last, what if we aren't visible by dinnertime? Or worse, what if we suddenly appear right in front of people?"

"We can always take dinner in my room if we aren't visible yet. Also, I'll bring my pouch. That way if either of us begin to show signs of appearing before we're ready, we can take another pill and make our escape unnoticed."

"Deal!" Millie announced exuberantly.

After Aylan was washed, she dressed in her clean clothes. Millie laughed out loud at the result. Aylan's clothes seemed to hang in the air as if being worn by someone, yet no body could be seen. "Interesting," Aylan said as Millie explained the source of her mirth. She decided that when Millie took her pill, she would also take another half just in case the first pill might wear off much sooner than the other. Millie picked a pill out of Aylan's pouch and sniffed it. The odour of the pill was strong and full of musk. She recoiled, turning slightly green.

"Plug your nose," encouraged Aylan, "It works pretty well to kill the smell and most of the taste." The two girls plugged their noses, placed the pills in their mouths and drank deeply from the pitcher to help them swallow back the thick muddy taste.

"Goodness," said Millie once she had swallowed her pill, "I thought the wretched thing might never go down!" She stared in Aylan's direction, but could not see her, and was relieved to know that her mistress' new clothes were no longer visible.

Aylan made sure to spread her pouches out on her belt, so that they would not be able to collide and make noise when she moved. "Before we get started," she announced, "I need to make a quick note." Millie watched as Aylan's notebook seemed to open on the desk by itself. The pages flipped and turned to a clean page, while her writing quill seemed to float in the air, dipping itself in the inkwell. It moved seemingly by magic as Aylan scribbled down what she knew of the pills so far. The top page fluttered lightly as Aylan blew across the drying ink and put her quill away.

"Ready!" she told Millie as she closed her book. "I have an idea of where we can go too, follow me!" she said as she threw open the door and proceeded down the hallway. After a few moments, Aylan realized that Millie wasn't with her and her doorway was still wide open. She returned back down the hall and called to her handmaid in a hushed impatient voice, "Millie? Why aren't you coming?"

"Um, Milady?" Millie answered, "I don't mean

to question your judgement, but how am I to follow you when I can't see where you are?"

"Oh! I hadn't thought of that." She admitted in surprise. "This *is* going to take some getting used to. Try listening to my footsteps. I will try to drag my heels a little. If we go outside, look for my footprints. I will tell you when I'm turning as long as no one is around. We don't want to scare more peasants into thinking that this castle is haunted."

Moments later, the two invisible girls were bustling through the open courtyard to the main entrance-way of the castle. They had taken the stairs down, crossed through the garden, and were approaching the portcullis of the outer wall. They turned before they reached it, heading through a stone doorway that led to the soldier's dormitory and fighting arena. They passed the kennel where all the hunting dogs slept, and continued to the arena. It was large and rectangular in shape except for its rounded corners. It had a sand floor and low stone walls, with seats all around the outside for spectators to come and watch jousting or other tournament events. Right now, the king's men were sparring and practicing swordplay and archery, kicking up dust as they moved.

Aylan and Millie walked around to the side of the arena so they would be able to get the best view of the knights hard at work. They sat on a wooden bench beside the stone wall bordering the ring and watched in awe as they saw Ormond himself mounted on a black steed. Directly in front of them, a section of the arena had been set aside for jousting practice. Ormond slowly made his way over to the end of the ring, taking a lance from his squire in one hand, and a shield in the other. He positioned his lance, flipped his helm's visor down to protect his face, and nodded in the direction of the other end of the ring. They looked down to the other end of the jousting run and saw a young knight, ready to face him. Visor already down and lance at the ready, he lowered his head, squared his shoulders and nodded back to Ormond.

The two men's horses galloped forward, hooves matching the girls' heartbeats that now pounded at an alarming speed. The opponents each raised their lances and shields. The deafening sound of the metal and wood colliding ensued as Ormond's lance exploded against the other knight's shield, littering the ground with splintered wood. The young knight seemed slightly unsettled as he completed his run to the opposite end of the arena. He righted himself in the saddle, turned his horse around and prepared for a new run. Ormond turned his mount as well and accepted a new lance. They nodded once again and keyed their horses forward. Another impressive blow followed, but this time the reverberating collision was against Ormond's giant shield. The girls could hear Ormond laugh a deep throaty chuckle as he passed them on his steed. The knight got a fresh lance and aimed it at Ormond once more. They charged at a blinding speed, lances levelled at one another, dust being kicked up by the horses' flying hooves.

If they had blinked, the two girls would have missed it. Both lances hit their marks, each with a mighty *crack!* Chunks of wood flew through the air in all directions from the impact. Ormond's horse continued to gallop as unbelievably, he was unseated and fell to the ground. The other knights sparring around the jousting run stopped fighting and approached to watch. The young knight that had been jousting with Ormond hopped down from his saddle, as two squires provided swords to the two men to finish the match. Ormond quickly righted himself, rising to his feet and taking his sword. The other knight's weapon wasn't much smaller than Ormond's, and the young man seemed to be having some difficulty wielding it. In fact, now that both were on the ground, the illusion of equal height that the horses had offered no longer existed. They could tell by looking at the two fighters how small the young knight really was. He couldn't have been more than a teenager. Compared to Ormond, he had a slender build and was a full head shorter than the general. Although the younger knight had caused the large man to fall from his horse, Aylan guessed that this would be a short fight.

Ormond fought as a practised soldier, using footwork to match his sword's strikes and parries. His opponent also used footwork, matching Ormond's blows with parries and dodges of his own. As the fight continued, the at-first awkward teen seemed to move faster, growing more confident. His blows became stronger and more sure. He moved faster and faster, and as they continued in a sort of dance with flashing swords, the tables turned. To this point, Ormond had had the offence, causing the teen to use purely defensive strategies. But somewhere along the way, the teen had gained the upper hand. His movements were so swift that as he dodged one of Ormond's heavy swings by rolling out of the way, he was able to turn quickly and catch Ormond in the back. Now the young knight was able to use offensive strategies, and his incredible speed was his advantage.

Though Ormond was much more muscled, his sword seemed heavier and slower to move. The teen's strikes came faster and faster until Ormond began to miss blocking a few hits. Each time the teen's sword hit Ormond's armour, a red mark was left behind. Ormond had one such mark on his back, and three on his front. The teen had two marks where Ormond had scored a hit. The young knight on the offensive, attacked again, pushed Ormond backwards as they fought. Their flashing swords clanged and clacked against each other with teeth rattling force until Ormond used his strength to push the teen back a few steps. Then the girls saw Ormond use a dirty trick. While the teen was still catching his balance, Ormond darted down, taking a handful of the ground's sand, and threw it viciously at the teen's eyes. A cloud of dust went up as the handful of dirt hit the boy's visor, and they could tell by the way his arm went up as if to wipe at his eyes that some had gone in, stinging his eyes and blinding him.

Ormond took his opportunity. He raced forward, sword aimed right at the teen's heart. The teen just stood there wiping at his eyes, and when Ormond was only two steps away, Millie cringed into Aylan's invisible shoulder, fearing the worst was about to happen. Aylan's heart went out to the young knight that had fought so gallantly, as Ormond's grip on his sword changed, ready to punch through the boy's armour. She watched in fear and horror as she realized that not one of the other knights that had come to watch was making a move to help him. Then, as Ormond took his final step toward his target, everything changed. The teen dropped and spun immediately, sticking his foot out as he turned. Ormond's sword pushed through thin air as the boy's outstretched foot swept Ormond's feet out from under him. Ormond's momentum caused him to fly through the air for a few feet before he crashed down heavily in the dirt, and skidded to a stop in a cloud of dirty smoke. As the dust began to clear, the boy calmly walked over to Ormond and held his sword at the larger man's throat, asking in a familiar voice: "Do you yield?"

Ormond began to laugh out loud and gave the young knight the kingdom's salute as he answered: "Well done Highness, yes I yield!" Aylan sat back in surprise as she watched the young knight first help Ormond up from the ground, then raise his visor to reveal the face of the prince. All those that had been standing around watching the match let out a loud whoop as they began to cheer and applaud. "I dare say that you could lead this army yourself!" offered Ormond as he clapped him on the back.

"I will leave the hard work to you Ormond, and stick to one day running a country," he laughed.

"In that case," announce Ormond jovially, "Everybody back to work!"

Chapter 11
~ How to Get a Bow ~

The two girls continued to watch the other men and boys that were practicing, but moved to a location closer to the exit. They feared that since it had been a while since they had taken their pills, they might start to become visible soon. They wanted to be close to the exit in case they had to make a quick get-away to avoid being discovered. On this side of the arena the boys were practicing the sport of archery. They all waited in a row for a command from Carn, then let loose their arrows. There were four giant targets set up along one of the walls that ringed the training arena. They were made of stacks of bales of hay covered with cloths that showed rings of red, blue and white. The arrows in the air flew quickly toward the targets, peppering them as they landed.

"Woo-hoo! That's four in a row, gents!" one boy gloated, nodding towards his arrow that had landed in the dead centre of the target's red circle: a perfect bulls-eye.

Aylan heard Millie sigh beside her. "Isn't he *wonderful?*" she gushed. Aylan nodded in awe before she realized that Millie wouldn't be able to see the nod.

"Yes, that's really quite something. I had no idea that the knights were so skilled at such a young age." Aylan whispered in awe.

Millie laughed out loud, quickly checking the volume of her voice. "These aren't knights yet, Aylan, these are only boys in training. Some of them are squires, others are merely those trying to enter the king's army, but serve no knight directly. You can tell them from the real knights because of their armour or equipment. The castle's training armour, swords, bows and other weapons do not bear the kingdom's insignia. No one is allowed to wear clothing or use equipment that has been marked with it until they've been officially accepted into the group of king's men. Their tunics have a symbol reflecting that. They are basically the same insignia, but they have no dragon's breath. When they are inducted into the king's army, they are said to have gained their fire." Aylan looked to Carn's armour with the dragon breathing fire, then at the boys' armour that had a dragon, but no flame.

"Wow," Aylan remarked, "how do you know so much about all of this?"

"See the smallish boy with the bow two sizes too big for him?"

Aylan looked at the archers and saw quite quickly an almost scrawny boy with a bow that clearly dwarfed him. The bigger boy that had hit the bulls-eye approached him and offered his assistance with the larger bow. He even offered the smaller boy his own shorter bow to use. The scrawny dark haired boy shook his head vehemently. "Yes, I see him," replied Aylan.

"That is my brother," she said matter-of-factly, "and the boy trying to help him is Bowregard. His father is one of the king's best archers, as was our father. They were friends, and so we have grown up together. Bowregard keeps trying to tell Thornton that he has to work up to a bow of that size. He's just not strong enough to pull back the bowstring. But," she sighed, "he refuses to use any bow except the one that belonged to our father. Bowregard is so patient with Thornton, and tries so hard to help him. Still, he is wasting his breath, Thornton won't bend."

"It sounds like Bowregard is a good friend," Aylan announced as she sized up the larger boy. He had a straight nose, pointy chin, wide forehead and loose red hair cropped to the ears. His broad shoulders were a little too wide for his tunic, and she could see that he had a healthy set of muscles.

"Yes, a good *friend*." Millie agreed, sighing again.

Aylan couldn't help but detect a hint of bitterness in Millie's voice. "I take it you wish he was more than a friend?" she hedged.

"I wish he wouldn't see me just as Thornton's sibling that happens to work at the castle where he practices being a knight. I wish he would see me for what I am, a *girl*."

"Maybe he just needs to have his eyes opened to how special you are." Aylan suggested. "I have another idea, come on!" she added.

The two girls made their way out of the arena, past the barracks and kennel, back into the fragrant garden. They started down a row that contained rose bushes. As the aroma of roses surrounded them, Aylan surveyed the area to see if anyone was looking in their particular direction, and quickly cut a single rose with her dagger. "What are you doing?" Millie gasped.

"We have to be careful now, people will be able to see the rose." Aylan warned, a smile in her voice. "Keep an eye out for people afoot."

"Where are we going?" asked Millie desperately as she saw Aylan's footprints begin to kick up dust in the warm dry air as they lead back towards the arena where the boys were.

Aylan just giggled in response. "Come on!" she urged.

Instead of going to the arena though, Aylan left the main path and took the smaller one that led to the barracks where the boys slept. She entered quietly, telling Millie "Shhh." Grit crunched lightly on the floor as they walked down one row of beds, and started down the next. "Which do you think belongs to Bowregard?" Aylan asked.

"I'm not sure, although Thornton did make mention of it being next to his. Thornton always keeps a likeness of father under his pillow. We can look for that. Also, we can rule out any bed that doesn't have a quiver. They generally leave them with their things unless they are travelling out of the castle to practice."

The two girls looked under pillow after pillow of all of the bunks with a quiver. They noticed that the beds seemed to be organized by archers, fighters, and riders. This made their work easier and quicker. As they felt under the soft linen pillowcases, they found that many beds held illustrations or letters from families, siblings or parents. Three quarters of the way down a row, Millie exclaimed: "I found it!" They searched the beds on either side of Thornton's and found that Bowregard too had a portrait of his family. "That's the one," Millie acknowledged, "I recognize his da." Aylan lay the sweet-smelling rose on the pillow of Bowregard's bed and put her hands on her hips, nodding in satisfaction.

"There!" she said, "Now he'll at least know to keep his eyes open!"

"Milady!" Millie gawked, "I can see you nod!"

Aylan looked closely at where Millie should be standing, and saw a flicker as Millie moved.

"I can see you too!" Aylan exclaimed as they heard a group of footsteps approaching from outside.

"Ooh, what are we to do?" Millie lamented.

"Quick!" Aylan responded, "Under the beds!"

The two girls dropped just as the door was

flung open and a group of boys strutted into the room. Their loud banter and footfalls on the wooden floor were enough to cover up the sound of Aylan and Millie scuttling under two of the beds. The girls fought the urge to sneeze as the dust from the floor tickled the inside of their noses. The conversation of the boys grew louder as they approached the girls' hiding spots.

"I don't care that I'm small!" a high voice insisted, "This bow was all that my father ever used, and if it was good enough for him, it shall be good enough for me too!"

Thornton, Millie silently mouthed to Aylan from her place under the bed.

The voices grew closer as the group of boys crossed the room. "But you have to acknowledge the fact-"

"Hey, Bow!" one of the other boys interrupted.

"Just a sec," Bowregard replied, then turning back to Thornton he continued, "that your father was a larger boy than you are. Father keeps trying to tell you-"

"Bow!" the other voice insisted again.

"Just one second, Trembleton, I'm talking to Thorn." He scolded, continuing to address Thornton again. This time the other boy tried to let him go on for a while without interrupting again. "Your da was almost six feet tall by the time he was twelve years old. You're right, it was all your da ever used, but that's because it fit him. You wish to be a great archer like him, but you'll never reach your potential unless you use the tools right for you. Besides-"

"By the shields of the army of Ormond, Bowregard, look at your pillow!" Trembleton finally bellowed.

There was a sound of clothes shifting and

voices falling silent momentarily as the boys turned to look at Bowregard's bed. "Ooh, who's the girl, Bow?" Thornton asked.

"Yeah right guys, very funny, which one of you planted the rose?" Bowregard interrogated.

"Wasn't me, Bow," Thornton said.

"Nor I," Trembleton pledged, "I swear!"

"It must have been one of the hand-to-hand guys," Bowregard pondered as he picked up the rose and lifted it to his nose.

"Couldn't have been," Trembleton reasoned, "we were the last ones out of here before practice began because we had to come back for my bracer. There was nothing on your bed then, I'd swear to it."

"So fess up Bow, who's the lucky lady?" Thornton pressed.

"None that I know of," Bowregard said. "But I'd like to find out."

"Ah, I love an intrigue!" Trembleton hollered excitedly. "Alright gents, it's time to find out who it is that has captured Bow's heart!"

"Hold now my friends, it will take a lot more than a single rose to capture any part of me, including my heart," Bowregard assured them.

Under the bed Aylan giggled quietly to herself as Millie once more mouthed to her: *what have you gotten me into?*

"Did you just hear something?" Bowregard asked quickly on edge as Thorn flopped down onto his bed. Under his weight, the bed sagged, slighting crushing Millie and sending her breath out in a whoosh.

"No, but maybe you're hearing the voice of your true love!" Thornton quipped. Bowregard socked him immediately in the arm.

"Ow! That hurt, and you know what Carn always says," Thornton grumbled, then continued in a pretty good imitation of Carn's voice: "No quarreling! If we fight amongst ourselves, the enemy might as well sit back and let us do their job for them!"

Trembleton laughed as Bowregard knelt between the beds where the girls hid, poised as a knight would, "Please forgive your humble servant, Thorn, I meant no harm!" he announced. Millie held her breath, not wanting to give away their hiding place as Bowregard's knee rested on the floor five inches from her face. Then just as quickly as he had knelt, Bowregard was up, pulling Thornton into a headlock. "Oh you know I would never hurt a hair on your head. Besides, your sister would kill me if I did, and I'd never get to watch you shoot your father's bow."

"C'mon Bow, do you really think she could take you?" teased Trembleton.

"Definitely," replied Bow. Under her bed, Aylan winked as Millie's face went bright red.

"Perhaps *she* is your perfect match then!" Trembleton put forth.

"Alas," Bowregard cried dramatically, throwing his arm across his eyes, "my heart already belongs to another. She of the red rose!" Under the bed, Aylan's smile widened.

Chapter 12
~ Spying a Spy ~

The next day, Aylan spent most of her time locked up in Lazelan's workroom. As she worked, Lazelan absentmindedly picked up her notebook and started flipping through it. When he got to the entry about the brown invisibility pills, he stopped her. "Where did you get all this information? This is great!" Aylan felt she could trust Lazelan, so she confided in him the whole story of the previous day. She added her thoughts about making pills for the soldiers. She described the possible setbacks of the water and the issues with the sound of the clanging armour and smell of the soldier's sweat or other odours. Lazelan was thoroughly impressed, and laughed out loud at the thought of the two servants running down the hallway shrieking about a ghost. She asked him about the red marks on Ormond and Oslan's armour during their fight in the arena, and how Ormond could attack with a shot that might kill the prince by running him through the heart.

"When the knights are training, I treat their armour with a spell. It fortifies its strength so that a weapon cannot accidentally punch through. Also, each time a weapon of any kind hits it, a red mark appears so that they can keep track of their hits. This helps Ormond later show his pupils how they are attacking, and how to improve."

Lazelan flipped through some more of her pages, pensive for a few moments, and then added: "We'll have to order a new basin for you from the potter. Until it arrives though, you can use one from here. I have a few extras due to the seriousness of some of the potions we make and use." Lazelan told her.

"The first time I made an invisibility pill, I was

in university," Lazelan began as Aylan went back to work, and Sasha listened. "A few of my classmates and I took our pills to the local pub after classes were done for the day. Like you, we weren't sure what effect the pills would produce, so we thought it might be useful to stay in a pack in case first aid was needed after consuming them. Once the first of us had taken his pill, the rest of us quickly followed suit. You should have heard the serving wench curse our names when she looked over and it appeared that we had all left without paying for our food!" he chuckled and Aylan grinned. "I'm afraid we made matters worse though when we decided to all carry our plates and mugs back to the bar for her. The poor lass fainted right away."

"Tsk, tsk," Sasha said, shaking her head as if at an incorrigible child.

Lazelan cleared his throat while he looked at Sasha sideways. "We made sure to leave a rather large tip for her to find upon waking up."

"Or they would have," Sasha continued, "If they could have seen which coins they were leaving on the table."

Lazelan looked at Aylan sheepishly. "I'm afraid she's right. We tried to leave her a pile of silver for her to find. Unfortunately as you know, everything you wear and carry when taking the pill also turns invisible. I must admit that we didn't really know what we left behind. All of the coins of our kingdom were the same size and shape. All we knew was that it seemed to us to be a fair sized pile of coins."

"What they discovered upon checking their purses the next day," Sasha interjected, "Was that all that was missing was copper. Each of them by some fluke had left her a pile of copper, which would not even have paid for their drinks." She laughed.

"So what happened?" Aylan pressed.

"Oh, we learned our lesson alright. We went back the next day to confess to the barkeep. He made us wash dishes for a week to make amends. It ended up being a good thing though. One night while working there, an old blind man came up to the bar and went to pay for his drink. He held out his handful of coins and asked the barkeep to pick out which coins were appropriate. I asked him how he knew that the barkeep had taken the right amount of coins. The man said that he wouldn't know, he relied on trusting people, but not all people were trustworthy. He told us that if he were the ones making the coins, he would put markings on the edges so that people who couldn't see could tell the coins apart. We used his idea in class for a project. Those of us who could use magic were given the goal of doing so in a way that would benefit those in the kingdom over a period of time."

"Why over a period of time?" Aylan interrupted.

"Because then no student could simply create a pile of money for the king or professor and say that it would improve their lives. We were to help many people for the long term." Lazelan recounted.

"The blind man helped them, he was really quite clever." Sasha piped up in her trilling voice.

"He helped us devise a system whereby each coin would have a different type of edging or mark. It wasn't enough to have coins that were different sizes, because you might not know which size it was if you had no other coins to compare it to. We used magic to change the blind man's coins. We put ridges on edges of the silver coins, left the coppers smooth and round and put spaced out dots on the edge of the gold coins, like the four points on the compass."

"That's brilliant!" exclaimed Aylan, smiling.

"Aye, but it only helped the one man, and only until he changed coins once with a shop keeper. As soon as he had new coins, he would have the same problem. So we went to the king with the university's permission. We brought our blind friend with us, and did a demonstration in front of the court. He showed the king that he could count out and find the correct money for any amount the king named. He was tested and re-tested. Some of the nobles spoke up and added how this would help their aged fathers and mothers."

"This is the best part!" Sasha said.

"Unbeknownst to us, the royal family had had a daughter that was blind. She sought her independence, but could not even go to the marketplace on her own. The king made a decree that all money was to be changed over to our new system. The blind man was given a job to oversee the whole operation, and test that all the coins had been marked in a way that could be read. The king was so impressed that he also spoke to the university which then offered me my post there. The word spread, and now many kingdoms are using our method of marking coins so that even if blind people travel to other kingdoms, they will not be taken advantage of."

"I always wondered about that." Aylan remarked, removing a coin from her pouch and looking at the edges that bore Lazelan's marks.

*   *   *

After finishing her potion-making for the day, Aylan returned to her room. She was looking forward to the next day, when she and Lazelan were to go on their first trip together to the king's forest to learn about new herbs she'd never seen.

"Milady, look!" came Millie's anxious voice from the balcony. Aylan set down her things and walked outside into the sunshine to meet her.

"What's going on?" Aylan asked.

"Look, down there in the garden!" Millie hissed.

Aylan looked to where Millie was pointing and spied Bowregard and his two friends among the long shadows checking the rose bushes for the empty stem that had been cut. He looked up at the exact moment that Millie pointed down at him. Millie turned crimson and dropped her arm to her side.

"That'll teach you to spy while you're visible!" Aylan teased.

"Millie, is that you?" Bowregard called up to her.

Aylan thought quickly. Putting on the airs and superior voice of a noble, she lifted her chin and replied: "Aye, this is my lady in waiting. She came to alert me that someone was skulking around in the garden, spying on our rooms!" Aylan acted taken aback. "Just what *is* the meaning of this?" Aylan demanded. "Do you always make it a habit to spy on ladies while they are preparing for dinner?"

In the garden, Bowregard sputtered as Trembleton guffawed loudly enough for the two girls to hear. "Aw Millie, it's just us!" Thornton called back to her.

"I would ask you not to fraternize with my servant while she is *supposed* to be working. If you must speak to her, I would invite you to stop by *after* dinner once her chores are done." Aylan said while pretending to admonish Millie.

"Ooh, thank you for your *permission*!" called Trembleton sarcastically.

"You're welcome!" responded Aylan immediately. "We will expect you gentlemen no later than eight o'clock! Come now, Millie!" she said dramatically, pulling Millie back inside and banging the balcony doors closed behind them.

Inside, Millie rested her back against the wall catching her breath. "That was unbelievable! Where did you learn to act like that? I actually thought you were a noble for a moment!"

"I learned a lot while watching my aunt. I was pretty much sent to her house each year for a bout of finishing school. If I had to, I could appear as a queen!"

Millie began to laugh, and then stopped short. "Wait a minute. You just invited them here, tonight!"

"I suppose I did. I guess we had better get this place cleaned up!"

Down in the garden, the boys still stood looking at each other in shock. They had just come out here to look at the rose bushes, and now they had somehow been roped into a visit with a noble that seemed to be quite haughty.

Chapter 13
~ Reflecting the King ~

Millie started cleaning every nook and cranny in the girls' tiny room. She piled the broken pieces of the basin on the desk in a neat stack. When Aylan asked her about it, Millie replied: "Well we can't have the boys here without a basin! I'll do what I can to glue it back together." Aylan nodded and excused herself to go talk to the prince.

She sought him out in his chambers where she had first met him. She approached his door, listened for a moment and hearing sounds coming from within, knocked.

Inside, the prince was changing for dinner. He was currently attempting to choose between a blue tunic and a purple one. "Who is it that wishes to enter?" he called.

"It is just I: Aylan, Prince Oslan." She called back, startled at his manner of speech.

The prince felt his heart speed a little at the sound of her voice. "Peculiar," he mused. He found himself rushing to dress then, absentmindedly choosing the tunic that matched her eyes. He ran to his mirror and tried to comb his fingers through his hair to make himself look more presentable. From in the hall he heard Aylan grumble "Oslan, I fear I might grow a beard as long as your father's before you open the door!"

Oslan rushed to the door and waited for the tell-tale heat to leave his cheeks before opening it. She entered, teasing him by doing an impersonation of his last words to her: "Who is it that wishes to enter?"

Once again the prince flushed. "I have to speak like royalty when you're not around, you know. Do you think they let just anyone sit on the throne?" he sputtered in mock horror. "Please! We have standards!"

"Well you always look like a prince. You look well in that tunic. Blue suits you, Oslan."

Oslan changed the subject, "What brings you to see me, Aylan?"

Aylan put on a sad face and sniffed. "I thought friends were *supposed* to visit each other. Prince, you told me to call you Oslan! You *said* we were friends!" she wailed in a cracking voice, covering her face with her hands and turning away from him.

The prince, distressed, tried to placate her. "Of *course* we are friends, of *course* I meant it!" he soothed as he took a step toward her. Only then did he hear her soft giggle muffled by her hands. "Aylan, you are going to be the death of me one day, as I fear you will make me die of a heart attack as a reaction to one of your jokes."

"Oh no, Prince, I will be your mage, I will save you, not kill you!" she insisted, smiling.

"Perhaps we should change your job to court jester instead, just in case," he teased.

"Nah, magic is better. In fact, that is the real reason I came to see you today."

"Oh?" he asked, "Are you having any difficulties? I see Lazelan hasn't managed to cure you of your pranks, but perhaps you have caused him to crack a smile?"

"As a matter of fact it is going swimmingly, and I have in fact had Lazelan smiling more often than not," she informed him.

Intrigued, the prince asked: "How did you manage that?"

"Lazelan thinks I'm his star student. Apparently magic comes naturally to me, or so he thinks. At first it was really difficult, but I got used to telling the different plants and oils apart, and now I just find it easy."

"Excellent!" Oslan said approvingly. "But jokes aside, I get the feeling that is not the reason that you came to see me today. I don't see you as the type to come just to boast."

"Well," Aylan started, and told him of Millie's situation. She recalled the afternoon's blunder, when Millie pointed out Bowregard in the garden with his friends and the ensuing invitation.

The prince laughed gently. "It would have been something to see you act as a lady! You must show me how you spoke. Quickly, let's have it!" So Aylan set her voice just right and started admonishing the prince. "Oslan, you really should speak to your servants! This place is disgusting. I think I might see some actual dust in your fireplace!" The prince howled with laughter.

"Yes, yes, it was all good fun," Aylan admitted.

"Bowregard is one of my friends, and he is a stubborn sort," confided the prince, "I know Thorn and Trembleton too, they are all good lads. They all practice archery while I practice my swordplay in the arena," he told her. "I don't know if Millie will have much luck though. Bowregard is a little obsessed right now. Apparently, he has a secret admirer. He found a rose on his bed after practice yesterday, and he has been going crazy trying to find out who left it for him!"

No kidding, she thought. Aylan turned serious. "This is the problem though. They are coming to see us tonight! I have a favour to ask of you...and of your sister." Oslan listened while Aylan told him her plan.

*   *   *

Bowregard found the prince walking the hallways of the castle. "Prince Oslan, may I have a word with you?"

"Of course, what is it?" he replied.

"There is a noble in the palace, a young girl. Well, a girl our age actually. Maybe you know her?"

"Oh, I'm not sure, Bow. There are so many nobles that pass in and out of the palace," he answered in a pensive tone.

Glumly, Bowregard continued: "Anyway, she has invited Thorn, Trembleton and I to her quarters this evening. The only thing is, I can't figure out how it happened. I don't recall accepting the invite, but there it is, we're expected. Perhaps I just won't go."

"A lady should never be kept waiting!" the prince admonished. "Part of being one of the king's men is that we reflect the king. How would it look if the king's men aren't trustworthy to keep their word?"

"But I was thinking," pleaded Bowregard, "what if you were to send for me. That way we would have a valid excuse for departing or not arriving in the first place."

"I'm afraid I can't help you, Bow. I already have an engagement with my sister this evening. You'll just have to face the dreaded maid all by yourself. Perhaps she is the one that left you that rose."

"Ha!" Bowregard barked, "she would never set foot in the garden, or anywhere her gown could possibly get dirty."

"I very much doubt that." The prince laughed under his breath.

"Pardon me?" asked Bowregard, who had not heard him.

"I asked what colour gown she was wearing,"

recovered the prince.

"I don't rightly know, Highness, she was up on the balcony, so I could not see." Bowregard acknowledged. "I suppose we will have to attend then. If we don't show up for practice tomorrow, you'll know why!"

The prince raised his eyebrows as if to say "oh?"

"Eaten by the dragon lady!" he replied smugly.

Chapter 14
~ The Yellow One ~

"Hurry, go get ready!" Tanyan urged.

"I cannot thank you enough!" said Millie again, beginning to exhaust the princess's patience.

"Believe me, you have thanked her about forty times more than enough," Aylan insisted, "Now go and put one on, they will be here soon!"

Once Millie bustled out of Aylan's room, Aylan, Oslan and Tanyan all breathed a sigh of relief. Tanyan was Oslan's middle sister, and was older than him by eleven months. She had dark ringlets that fell down her back to her waist, and had the same colour of eyes as the prince. Aylan found her to be very sweet, if a little impatient, but she had good-naturedly heard out Aylan's plan. She had not only agreed to go along with it, but even asked Millie in to see her to make sure she picked dresses that would accentuate her skin colour and features.

There was a knock at the door. Aylan answered it by winking at the prince and calling out the same phrase he had used with her: "Who is it that wishes to enter?"

From on the other side of the door, they heard: "Sheesh, is she serious? Oof!"

"It is none other than the three you are expecting, Milady." Bowregard called through the door.

"You may enter!" allowed Aylan in a regal voice. Tanyan stifled a giggle as the door swung open to reveal Bowregard and Thornton in the lead. Trembleton stood behind them rubbing his ribs and looking crossly at Thorn." As the boys surveyed the room, a look of surprise crossed Bowregard's face. The prince and his sister seemed to be deep in conversation with the lady that had summoned them, and she was dressed as a boy in tunic and hose.

"Do join us," insisted the prince, "This is Aylan. Her handmaiden will be here shortly to show us another dress."

"What dress?" Thornton asked.

"Aylan is trying to decide on a style of dress that will suit her, so I decided on a fashion show!" Tanyan declared exuberantly.

The boys looked around the room. Seeing that Tanyan had seated herself on the bed cover beside Aylan, and Oslan had chosen a stool nearby, Bowregard quickly drew up the other stool beside him. Trembleton and Thorn sat cross legged on the room's round rug, waiting for the show. "This is a bit of a cramped space for a fashion show, isn't it?" Trembleton asked.

"Of course it would be in the great room if we wanted any noble in the kingdom to be able to see the princess' gowns as well and have a tailor make each lady the same dress," said Aylan. "However, part of what makes a dress so special is that no one else has one quite like it. Therefore, Princess Tanyan was very generous and allowed for this private viewing for me."

Just then the sound of bustling fabric came from the hall. They all waited expectantly in the lightly scented room, eyes on the door. Nothing happened. The door remained closed and the bustling stopped. The prince cleared his throat loudly to acknowledge that they were ready and waiting. Still no one opened the door to let themselves in.

"You may enter!" said Aylan magnanimously.

Out in the hall, Millie was all but hyperventilating. She was standing outside the door wearing a beautiful gown. Aylan had spent hours that afternoon braiding her hair and putting it up in intricate ways that Aylan had observed in her aunt's manor. She was so nervous, she thought she might faint. When Aylan cleared her voice and called: "You may enter!" again, she knew she had to go in. After the huge steps her mistress had taken for her, she couldn't let her down. Millie took one more deep breath and prepared to walk through the door.

Inside the room the royalty was getting impatient. Oslan finally said: "I will go and see what is taking that girl so long!" He took the few steps to the door and opened it, revealing Millie standing in the doorway.

"Wow!" came an appreciative exclamation from those gathered in the room. Millie glimmered and shimmered from head to toe in gossamer tyrian purple. Her hair was pulled back from her face in intricate braids that criss-crossed to the crown of her head where they all joined together forming a bun. The bodice of the dress had its own criss-crossing pattern that mirrored her hair, and the lower half floated gently to the ground. No one could deny that she was beautiful. But instead of paying attention to the dresses, after Millie's initial entrance, Aylan secretly watched the boys. She wanted to see Bowregard's honest reaction, and was pleased to see that every time Millie entered, his eyes seemed to be glued to her in wonder.

Millie tried on dress after dress, and at one point, Oslan leaned over to her, startling her out of her thoughts by saying "You should pick that one, it would look wonderful on you." Aylan glanced at Millie to see that she was wearing a blue-turquoise dress that had shimmered like the purple one. It had gathered material at the waist that parted at the front of the skirt revealing another skirt underneath. She nodded appreciatively. "It's very pretty," she remarked. Next, Millie appeared in a yellow gown, plainer than the rest, with no excess fabric. This one was simple, but Millie seemed almost to glow in it, and a smile unconsciously spread across Bowregard's face.

Then there was a burgundy dress that showed quite a bit of shoulder. Oslan looked over at his sister, surprised. She blushed back nervously, telling him that it was a new dress she hadn't yet worn for her coming-out ball. He seemed to consider her as a young woman for the first time, and told her that he believed that she would be stunning in it. That seemed to please her, and the smile that grew on her face remained there until the royalty had left for the evening.

Eventually, Millie ran out of dresses. All of the boys had a different opinion as to which Aylan should choose, and although Aylan detested dresses altogether, she couldn't help speculating what she herself might look like in them. She told herself that it was purely for curiosity's sake, of course. As part of the façade, she made a show of pretending to choose, and made sure to ask Millie's opinion when Bowregard didn't speak up. Millie agreed with the prince that the turquoise-blue one would be best for her. She asked Tanyan to have a tailor make one up for her post haste. Tanyan said it would be done with a wink to her and the prince.

The boys finally left for the evening with Oslan and Tanyan. "Did you notice how quiet he was, Milady?" Millie asked afterward. "It is true that I was away a lot, changing into yards of fabric, but he seemed to say not a word the whole time I was there! What do you think it means?"

"I believe that he was purely stunned into a pleasant silence. But I will find out for sure tomorrow."

"What are you going to do now?" Millie asked anxiously. "We've already gone to such lengths to get him to notice me. What if he was silent because he was bored into thinking of his afternoon's battle maneuvers. Or even worse, perhaps he was thinking of the girl with the rose?"

"Millie! You *are* the girl with the rose!" Aylan reminded her.

"Yes, Milady, but he doesn't know it. What if he was so bored tonight that he will run screaming in the opposite direction next time we meet lest he get roped into another fashion show?"

"I will find out tomorrow." Aylan repeated.

"But how will you find out? What occasion do you have to even speak to him?" Millie pressed nervously.

"It's simple," Aylan said, "He never told us which dress he liked best."

As the girls sat together; Millie on the floor and Aylan on the bed behind her, Aylan prepared to take down Millie's plaited hair. They talked and laughed while they worked, and as Aylan unbraided, Millie brushed out each strand till her hair was tangle-free. "Did you hear something?" Millie asked suddenly as she froze. A timid knock at the door three times, then a voice just above a whisper: "Milady?" Aylan nodded to Millie to open the door, but Millie only shook her head, whimpered and mouthed *Bowregard.*

With a sigh, Aylan got up to open it herself. "Honestly, Millie, you're going to have to get over this aversion to boys if you ever intend to get married!"

Millie's face dropped into an expression of astonishment as if she hadn't actually thought of getting married before. Perhaps she had thought of marriage, but had never put a face into the fantasy before. There had never been a boy around before when she thought of one day getting married. But now there was. Now Bow's face swam into her daydream as Aylan opened the door.

Bowregard stood alone on the other side of the doorway and bowed low. "Please excuse the late hour, Milady," Bow started, "But I only just left the prince and his sister. I realized that I hadn't given my opinion on the dresses."

"Yes?" Aylan asked, noticing that he fidgeted nervously and was staring at Millie. "Which one did you think was best?"

"I think you looked beautiful in them all-" he choked off in mid-sentence and started again. "That is to say the gowns were all beautiful and made Millie look like a princess, and it's hard to picture you in a dress while you wear a tunic, Milady," he stumbled at Aylan's budding annoyance at the mention of her clothes. "I...I...I liked the yellow one." He managed at last. He bowed again quickly, turned and walked off.

Millie slowly backed up, slid down the wall, and collapsed in a nerve-sprung heap on the floor.

"Well, given that he was looking over my shoulder at you the whole time he was speaking, I'd say you seem to have left quite an impression on him!" congratulated Aylan.

Chapter 15
~ It Came in the Night ~

As Aylan slept that night, she had a fitful dream. In it, Carn was running after her, but this time he wasn't in pursuit. In her dream she ran with Carn away from something much more menacing. She didn't know what she was running from; just that she didn't want to stop to find out. They were moving swiftly through a forest that was full of dark green vines, leaves and ferns. The trunks on the huge trees towered dark brown all around them. It was a very old forest; the trees so big around that Aylan could not have wrapped both arms around one. They followed a path that zigged and zagged around bushes and plants she began to recognize. There was some lizard root, one of the ingredients in her invisibility spell, and the rest oddly enough seemed to be growing around it. There were other patches of different vegetation all growing together, as if they were meant to be made into a magic potion, paste or dust. She started slowing and heard an urgent familiar voice ahead. "Come on Aylan, this way!" It was Lazelan.

She followed the sound of his voice until she saw him standing on the path ahead of them. Relief at seeing him flooded her, but the fear of what might be pursuing them still made her feel frantic. Lazelan was amongst a great heap of rubble. "You can hide us, but you have to work quickly," he told her.

"I will go back down the path a ways and fend off the beast!" Carn called to her as Aylan caught up to Lazelan.

She looked around at what appeared to be curved and flat shards of broken rock. The pieces themselves were large, some knee-high, others waist high. It looked like a mighty boulder had exploded.

"You can help here, Aylan. These pieces of rock were once a mighty shelter. You can rebuild it."

"How?" Aylan asked, astonished, "I bet that I would not be able to lift but one of these rocks, let alone assemble all of them into a fortress. Besides, how am I supposed to know which piece goes in which location, and how can I make them stick together?"

"Think of it like a puzzle. This "fortress" as you call it was like a cave, so the inside will be smooth stone and the outside rough. Move them with your will. Like a conductor conducting a group of musicians, point to your chosen stone, feel it, and move it. Deep inside, you will find your core energy. Tap into it and use it if you can." He instructed.

Aylan chose a rock that was not too large. It was about the length of her forearm, was wide, and had a pointed tip. She raised her hand in its direction, curling her thumb and fingers in until she pointed with just one. She closed her eyes and looked within her own mind. She could picture an electric ball of energy. She tried to shoot that energy out from the tip of her finger toward the rock to lift it. She heard an explosion. Opening her eyes, she saw Lazelan stare in disbelief. There was white dust in his hair and particles flew around the area. The rock she was trying to move had been decimated. The place where it had sat lodged in the ground was now a steaming blackened crater in the earth. She quickly tucked her finger back in feeling guilty and frightened at her own power. "What happened?"

"You killed it." Lazelan said softly while looking at her, joking for the first time.

Startled, Aylan literally forgot to laugh. "Ok, I won't do that ever again."

She was brought out of her shock by the sound of a deafening roar. Fear gripped her.

Lazelan grasped her by the arms, focusing intently on her. "You've got to try!" he coached, "Just move it, *gently.* While you channel your energy, say the word *fli,* it means levitate in the language of magic." The fact that Lazelan took a few good steps away from her and the next rock she looked at, did not escape her notice, making her feel even more nervous.

This time she extended all her fingers and held her hand palm up, like a shelf. She held her hand in such a way that the rock shard appeared to be sitting on top of her hand. She closed her eyes and focused on that ball of energy in her mind once more. She tried to picture some of the electric tendrils flowing down her neck, through her shoulder and down her arm to the tips of her extended fingers. She pushed it gently further until it stretched to under the boulder. "Fli," she said as she slowly lifted her arm while it tingled with the energy.

"That's it!" Lazelan cried.

Startled out of her concentration, Aylan's eyes flew open just in time to watch the rock fall from where she had lifted it in the air. It came crashing down, but did not break. She felt the electric energy snap back into her mind to rejoin the glowing orb.

She heard the clear ringing *shing* of Carn's blade being drawn further down the path. Desperate, she tried again. Now that she had found the orb within her mind, she found she didn't need to close her eyes to tap into it. It was easier to concentrate without all of the visual distractions of the forest when her eyes were closed, but now she could work from feel. She once again sent the energy out of her flat hand to slide under the piece of stone. She was able to lift it and even move it sideways by separating her fingers like a claw that was grasping all sides of the rock. She turned it until it was able to fit against another piece the right way, lowering it until it came to rest. With Lazelan's help, she picked and chose the shards one by one, fusing them together in the right spots with magic from her other hand. When it was all done, it made a flat roofed dome. There seemed to be one jagged hole where the piece she demolished would have fit. It suited them better that way though; now there was a way to wriggle in. She called to Carn, who came running back up the path. The three ducked inside the newly reformed cave, and Aylan woke up.

The room was dark, and Aylan could only see the silhouettes of things by the starlight and moonlight coming in from the balcony. Millie lay asleep on her bedroll, unmoving, but breathing steadily deep in sleep. There was a knock at the door. Aylan looked toward the sound, wondering what was happening that someone would disturb her at this early hour of the morning.

"Aylan, open up, I know you're awake!" Sasha whispered fervently.

Aylan crawled from her warm bed, wincing as her feet crossed from the rug to the cold flagstone floor. She opened the door to reveal Sasha in her nightdress, hair tousled from sleep. "It has happened." She said archaically over the candle she was carrying.

"What has happened?" asked Aylan, annoyed at this late night intrusion.

"You used magic!" Sasha gushed.

"I use magic every day," groaned Aylan, "Why must you come to my chambers in the dark morning before even the rooster wakes and announce it?" Aylan asked grumpily.

"No, you silly fool!" Sasha said kindly, "You

just used real magic for the first time. Not potions or powders or dark smelly pastes, I mean magic of the mind!"

"Sasha, I've been asleep. I can assure you that although I am quite fond of my teachings, I do not stay up all hours of the night doing nothing else. I happen to also be fond of sleeping." Aylan insisted.

With a wry smile, Sasha enquired as to the whereabouts of Aylan's basin. Aylan gestured to the basin by the pitcher with a look that said *where else would it be?* "No," Sasha pressed, "not the one Lazelan lent you. Where is *your* basin, the one that you attacked the unsuspecting servant with?"

Aylan was pretty sure that Sasha couldn't see her roll her eyes as she turned away from the candle light. "The pieces are over there on the-" she stopped in mid-sentence as she looked to the writing desk. Instead of the neat pile of shards Millie had given up on, her bowl sat, once again whole. It was upside down, and instantly she recognized the shape of the shelter in her dream. She hurried over to it. Sasha let herself in and followed close behind. Sasha set the candle down on the writing desk and picked it up. The bowl was perfectly whole again save for one missing shard by the rim on one side. Under the bowl was a small scorch mark in the wooden table and a small area covered in white dust.

"Whew, you're lucky that you didn't burn the castle down!" Sasha commented.

"I don't understand. How...?" Aylan was at a loss for words.

"I think it's time we go wake Lazelan. He can explain it better than I." Sasha said.

Sasha regained her candle as Aylan scribbled a quick note to leave for Millie so she wouldn't worry. Then they made haste to Lazelan's chamber carrying the reformed bowl as they went.

Chapter16
~ How Thyme Flies ~

Sasha and Aylan had spent the early hours of the morning showing Lazelan Aylan's newly repaired washbasin. He had her tell and re-tell her dream so that he could grasp just what had happened. They had parted for breakfast and to freshen up, taking the time to change into travelling clothes.

The hours leading up to lunch found Lazelan, Aylan, Millie, Oslan and Carn hiking and picking herbs in the king's forest. "Wow, déjà vu!" commented Aylan as the excursion reminded her of the forest in her dream, though now she felt safe.

"That is precisely why Carn accompanies us, just in case we are in need of protection," Lazelan commented, "In light of what happened last night, I thought it might put you more at ease."

"And what of Oslan?" she whispered, "Why did he come?"

"He came because he wanted to." Lazelan replied simply.

As they walked along forest paths, stopping to pick certain herbs, Lazelan quizzed Aylan on the passing vegetation and their uses. Aylan also took to pointing out different herbs to Millie, and passed them to her to carry once they were harvested. The trip was going uneventfully until both girls and Lazelan were hunkered down picking thyme. "This is a plant that is used in many ways," Aylan explained as they picked. "Knights sometimes carry it with them into battle to bring them courage. So now it is also used in some potions to bring courage to the drinker whether a knight or not. Also, it may be placed under the pillow at night to ward off nightmares."

The girls crouched back to back and settled

into the task of picking sprigs on either side of the path. Suddenly, Millie felt a sharp tug on her hair. "Ouch!" she exclaimed while turning to look at Aylan. "Milady, whatever did you do that for?"

"I have done nothing!" insisted Aylan as she turned to face Millie. "Keep picking, I see a nice clump about two steps that way." She pointed. Millie rubbed her head, confused, but continued to pick. Then the back of Aylan's hair was pulled so hard she fell onto her rump. "Millie!" she yelled, "What is the meaning of this?" But before she could go on, Oslan rushed to her side to help her up, and Carn began to laugh.

"There is your trouble, ladies," he said, pointing with his unsheathed sword at a low fork in a nearby tree, "We have an imp!"

They turned to see a little humanoid creature with wild brown hair, covering its mouth in laughter while clinging to the tree. Straining to hear, they could just pick out the sound of its quiet chittering laugh. "Are they safe to touch?" Aylan asked.

"Oh, safe enough," said Carn, "if you can catch one, that is. They are incredibly fast, and as long as it knows you are looking for it, it will stay a safe distance away."

"Hmm." Aylan seemed to ponder, but went back to her picking, this time just to the right of Carn. Following suit, Millie continued to harvest the herbs as well. Not a few minutes later, Aylan closed her eyes and tried to find her inner core. Like in her dream it was there. From where Lazelan now stood beside the prince, he watched as the little imp once again snuck up behind Aylan to make a move for her hair. The prince raised his hand to move to warn Aylan, but Lazelan silently stopped him. Placing a gentle hand on the prince's arm and shaking his head, he motioned for the prince to watch.   Slowly, a bunch of newly picked thyme appeared over Aylan's right shoulder. It suddenly swooped, unheld by any hand, towards the little imp, catching it unaware. The bunch of thyme smacked into it and carried it to a nearby tree, pinning it there. The imp struggled unhappily as Oslan and Lazelan clapped their hands. Millie spun, and shocked, asked: "What just happened?"

Lazelan answered that Aylan had just consciously used true magic for the first time. Carn looked surprised as a smile spread on his handsome face, touching his eyes. "But how did you know he was coming for you again?" he asked Aylan.

"Well good knight," Aylan replied jovially, "I watched him come near in your pretty, pretty armour. It is as polished as a mirror, and worked like a charm!"

Aylan approached the little man-thing and looked at it curiously as it struggled to get out from under the thyme. "Can we keep him?" she asked the prince.

"Not in my workshop!" Lazelan cried indignantly. "Do you know what kind of trouble these little fellows can get themselves into? Hair pulling is just the beginning. Even if you befriend him, he will still play his little tricks on you and all you own."

Aylan took hold of the imp gently, and released the magic in the thyme. The sprigs fell to the ground as Aylan lifted him to her. "What is your name?" she asked. It chittered back to her fiercely in what could only be assumed to be indecent language.

"Lazelan," the prince beseeched him. "Help her with this."

Lazelan rolled his eyes in perfect mimicry of Aylan, which caused all but Aylan to laugh. He approached Aylan and the imp, casting a spell over them both. Suddenly, the imp's impertinent yelling could be understood by her.

"Let me be! This isn't fair! You don't know how to play the game! Unhand me you giant troll!" he yelled at the top of his little lungs. Aylan told him that she was no troll, and asked it for its name again. It seemed startled that it could understand her. "Scritch", it replied as it stopped its struggling in her fist.

"Well Scritch," she said as she reached into her food pouch, "Good one, you got us. It is nice to make your acquaintance." She handed him a corner of her sandwich and petted him gently on the head.

"This is undignified," he grumbled, but ate the sandwich anyway.

"Alright," she allowed. "We have to go back to work now, and I would ask that you kindly leave us to our business. Go on now." She placed his feet on the ground and gingerly let go. He skittered off into the forest out of sight.

The five joked about the incident and about Aylan wanting to keep the imp as a pet. "Sure, old Scritch would be happy to fetch you your invisibility potion, however, he'd more than likely give you a potion that would turn you bright orange instead. Or he would fetch you your supper, but not before adding so much pepper to your stew that you would be sneezing for days!" Oslan jested. After multiple examples of how an imp might mess up any order given, she began to understand that the situation would certainly be better if they remained outdoors.

The small band of friends moved away from the thyme and continued to pick other herbs and ingredients. Unbeknownst to them, the imp was long gone. But now something else, something sinister, was watching them from afar.

Chapter 17
~ When Pigs Fly ~

The next Saturday brought with it a great deal of excitement for Aylan. She rose with sound of the chirping birds, having been barely able to sleep a wink through the night. She bathed by candle light in preparation for a special visit from her mother. After showing Millie how to prepare the bath with the right amount of essence of lilac, she climbed in. It was her mother that had taught her to add the scent of lilac to her bath. She had always done it for her when she was a child, and Aylan had fond memories of being pulled from the bath and wrapped in a warm towel on her mother's lap. Sitting there warm in her towel while being enveloped in both her mother's arms and the scent of lilacs that she and her mother shared while her mother towelled her off was where she felt the most secure. She reminisced about that feeling until it was time to climb out of her current bath and dress herself.

Millie silently approved of the bath and picked out a newer green tunic that Aylan's mother had not yet seen to impress her. In truth, a lot of Aylan's clothes were now new, as she had kept growing over the past few months in training. Aylan's birthday had passed a while ago, and the prince had ordered the tailor to make her two new outfits as a birthday gift. Millie and Aylan had gone to the tailor's so she could be measured, and the new clothes had arrived just this week right around the time of their run-in with the imp.

The purpose of this visit from their parents was a very exciting one indeed. On the way back from the king's forest, Oslan had invited them to attend a tournament that was to be held for any member of the kingdom that wished to enter. There would be events in jousting, sword fighting, archery, falconry, and many more. Lazelan would also be putting on a lights display in the sky at night with magic to start off the tournament after a grand feast. For the past two days, Aylan had helped him prepare mixtures that would light up the sky in different colours when ignited with a fire spell.

Millie was also excited to observe the tournament. Since the night that Millie had donned the princess' dresses, Bowregard had been finding excuses to run into Millie in the market, or pass her in the garden as of late. She was flattered by the extra attention, and Aylan could always tell when she had had a run in with him. Millie seemed to always return from these chance encounters with flushed cheeks and renewed energy, not to mention a huge smile to brighten her face. Today, Millie was going to present Bow with a token of her affection to wear while he competed. She tucked the soft piece of cloth into her bodice so it would be safe until she had the opportunity to give it to him.

Once they were dressed, the girls made ready to go eat breakfast. As they were walking to the dining room, a servant intercepted them and told Aylan that the prince requested her presence in his quarters. She bade goodbye to Millie, promising to meet her by the portcullis after her meeting with the prince so that they could await their parents together. Aylan went with the servant to Oslan's chambers. The servant announced her and she entered to find a harried prince in a panic. It only took a few moments of watching him pace, tug on his thick locks and listen to his ranting before she understood why he was wound up.

At the end of the tournament, which was to be a week long, there would be a ball. Each knight that won an event would have a parade of noble girls to choose from to dance the night away. More importantly, since the prince's thirteenth birthday, this would be the first chance of every eligible girl in the kingdom to present themselves to him as a potential wife. Every mother in the kingdom would be preparing their daughters of marrying age for the occasion. The king had decreed that Oslan must choose a girl to woo by his fourteenth birthday, or matches would be made for him. Any girl that was twelve or older was eligible, and many would be decked out in their best in order to catch his eye. The prince didn't stand a chance.

She found the whole thing rather amusing, and even though she was now among those girls that were of the right age to present themselves, she would not be getting dressed up like some princess in a fairy tale. Still, she felt a small pang of jealousy, which she squashed immediately, pushing it back down before it got a chance to fully rear its ugly head. Inwardly, she sighed, *those girls are going to make fools of themselves, falling over each other trying to curry his favour, and it's obvious he's not even interested.* Part of her was actually looking forward to the display, however, she felt for him too. His life was governed by many rules because of who he was.

"I need more time!" Oslan thundered as he paced, frustrated before Aylan. She found a seat in his anti-chamber, and watched him calmly as he grabbed two fist-fulls of his dark hair, causing them to stand on end. He turned to her that way, hands on his head, elbows sticking out, at a loss for words. She rose and approached him, taking his hands down from his hair. While she held his hands in one of hers, she used her other hand to smooth his locks back into place.

"While your father still rules, he gets to

make...well, the rules." She pointed out helpfully. Distracted momentarily, he realized that could smell a hint of lilacs coming off of her. He pulled his hands from her fingertips as he noticed his palms beginning to sweat, and took a few hasty steps away.

"But it isn't fair, it's *my* life!" he complained while sinking into his favourite chair across from where she stood. "I'm not ready to be bombarded with girls trying to claim me like a piece of land! I want to find love on my own, not have it shoved in my face!"

"Look at the bright side," she reasoned with him, "If you continue to try to pull all your hair out, the competition might thin as your hair does." The prince glowered at her, once again releasing his hair.

"Perhaps we could put your plan into action. This is what I propose..." And as Prince Oslan listened to his new mage, his eyes began to glow with delight at her brilliance.

*   *   *

Now ready by the palace gates, Millie and Aylan waited only slightly impatiently for their parents. Bowregard's parents had decided to accompany Aylan's mother so that they could watch Thorn and Bow compete against each other in the archery contest. Millie wanted to be the first one to greet them. Her own mother, like her daughter, was a servant in the castle, so she would join them at the feast once her kitchen duties were done. Hopping from foot to foot in their excitement, the girls saw four figures approaching the castle gates and ran out across the drawbridge to meet them. Bow's family greeted Millie warmly, the young child even reaching up for Millie to lift her. Aylan's mother beamed at her daughter as she told her about the upcoming sky-fire display.

Many people were starting to pour through the castle gates for the feast that was only an hour and a half away. Soon the food would be served, the market would be packed with people buying souvenirs of their trip, and knights would begin donning their armour in preparation for their first contest. The long sunlit hours of the summer provided an opportunity for the tournament to start following the feast while the light remained. After which, the fireworks would mark the beginning of the celebrations. Taverns would open and remain open for the duration of the week, while minstrels played music and people danced, drank, and made merry.

They entered the banquet hall in awe. Aylan's mother had never seen the inside of the palace, and its grandness made her stop just inside the doors to take it all in. The head table at the far end of the room was set up to view not only the guests, but also anyone entering the hall. The other heavy wooden tables were laid end to end in rows along each wall. The centre was left open to allow servers to come and go with food and drink, and afforded space for the royal jesters to entertain during the meal. Aylan stood looking with pride at the place she now considered home. The servants that worked in the castle, Millie included, had been hard at work hanging decorations and swaths of cloth to make the palace seem lavish and beautiful.

Once Aylan had plucked at her mother's sleeve to get her moving through the banquet hall, Millie led the small group to their seats at a long wooden table to the right of the king's head table. Here, Aylan would have an uninterrupted view of the banquet hall and of the royal family. Millie bustled off to help her mother, while the group sat admiring the decorations and watched the people milling here and there.

Aylan's mother noticed that although the hall was filling up, and most seats had been taken, there were still two spaces to the left of Aylan that were empty. As Millie passed by, serving them all drinks while they waited, they asked her about it. With a wink and a twinkle in her eye, Millie replied in a hushed matter-of-fact tone: "That is for your *cousin* that hasn't yet arrived." As Millie bustled off toward the kitchen, Aylan and her mother exchanged surprised glances. Then Lazelan was beside her, and on his arm a beautiful Sasha beamed. She leaned down to kiss Aylan on the cheek, exclaiming "Cousin!" Startled, Aylan floundered only for a moment before taking up the ruse. "Mother, you remember *Cousin* Sasha." She hinted with a wink to her mother.

Aylan stood to embrace Sasha, whispering in her ear "What are you doing here?" To which Sasha replied, "I couldn't stay away! You didn't really think I would sit alone in some dingy room all night missing the party, did you?" She shot a glance at Lazelan and added: "No offence to your laboratory, of course."

"None taken" he promised.

Aylan continued, turning to speak to her mother without skipping a beat. "And this fine gentleman is Lazelan, my teacher and mage of Endalwynndale. Lazelan, let me present to you my mother, Lorelyn."

Lazelan bowed and kissed the back of Lorelyn's hand. "Madam, I have found your daughter to be quite extraordinary."

Slightly flushed, her mother could only manage a quiet "Oh my!"

Lazelan turned his attention back to Sasha,

pulling her chair out for her next to Aylan.

At length, it was time for the feast to begin. Eight trumpeters entered the hall in two straight lines, stopping in the middle of the floor. They raised their trumpets in tandem and played a jaunty blast announcing the royal family to the guests. Everyone stood at their places and watched as the king, queen, Oslan and his three sisters, Talithan, Tanyan and Trindalynn entered the hall. This was the first occasion Aylan had had to view the queen. She was stunning and regal in a gold trimmed dress of red velvet. A glimmering crown sat atop her dark locks. Aylan could see that her three daughters resembled her very much, and hints of her face could be found in Oslan's features as well. They all walked to their places at the head table. The king and queen took the middle throne-like seats, followed by the three girls to the queen's left and Oslan to the king's right, closer to Aylan. As the king looked out over his people, the queen watched her children, and when Oslan's searching eyes found Aylan, a knowing smile appeared on the queen's beautiful face.

All of the knights, squires and other competitors then entered the hall to the peel of the trumpets and the cheer of the other guests. They stood behind their seats all together along the far side of the room were long benches had been set aside for them. The king stood and welcomed everyone. He made a pretty speech about the tournament to come and the mettle of the men and boys about to compete. Once he had finished to great applause, the servants began to bring out steaming plates of meats, root vegetables, and freshly baked bread. The smells of the piping hot dishes filled the hall, and babbling began amongst the crowd out of appreciation for the fine foods that made up the feast.

Aylan's mouth began to water with the scrumptious odours coming from the plates set before her. Then, it was time to eat. As Aylan's friends and family dined, she took every opportunity to talk to Millie while she brought things to their table. "Did you see Bow? He sits there," she pointed out as she directed Millie to the table in the middle of the opposite row.

"Milady!" Millie scolded, but turned to see and noticed Bowregard look away quickly. Millie blushed and bustled off to the kitchen with her tray. Bow's parents exchanged a surprised look at this new development.

On Millie's trip back into the kitchen, Sasha suddenly stiffened beside Lazelan, placing a hand on his arm. "Keep an eye on Millie," Sasha breathed, "Some pig of a man is about to try to harm her." Aylan turned her face from Sasha's to follow Millie's progress across the room. One of the men that had come from afar to compete in the tournament stood as she passed by him with her tray in hand. He pursued her, and she had almost made it out of the room before he caught Millie's arm.

"Now just where do you think you're going lass?" he asked. "Surely, you don't have to scuttle off so quickly, a pretty little thing like you." He advanced, causing her to back into the closest wall.

"Please sir, I have work to do," Millie managed shakily. But the large man's big meaty hand remained on her arm, detaining her. Millie's pleading eyes reached Aylan as she searched for help.

Both Bowregard and Oslan noticed the commotion and were up in a flash. Bow started to cross the hall, hands balled into angry fists. Oslan caused quite a commotion by leaving the head table and running straight across the hall to catch Bow before he reached the volatile situation. The prince caught up to the anger-filled teen and whispered the reminder in Bow's ear that should any fighting take place between any of the contestants, they would both be disqualified and stripped of their wins no matter when during the tournament the fight took place. Bow looked at the prince, and said: "Technically, the tournament hasn't begun yet." Oslan saw red hot determination in his eyes. The prince looked quickly to Aylan, who was observing the whole thing. Their eyes met, warm electricity, and Aylan acted. Quietly from her seat she focused her attention on the man. She found the source of her power and made a grabbing motion under the table. She pulled her hand back sharply and the man cornering Millie suddenly soared backwards, landing hard on his fat rump.

Millie's arm briefly jerked forward as the man flew back, until he finally released it in his surprise. A couple of women gasped at the sight and a few men shouted a muttled response of "Oi!" Now that the situation had been dissolved, Oslan allowed Bow to proceed, and he reached Millie quickly. Oslan saw to the man on the floor, a curse on his lips, but before he could say a word, King Eurilas rose and bellowed:

"What is the meaning of this?"

Oslan shot the man a warning glance and replied before the pig did. "It seems, Your Highness, that this man had a mind to harass one of our servants. But luckily for her, he seems to have tripped before any true harm could be done."

The king seemed to ponder this for a long moment, and then addressed the man in front of the court and all competitors. "You must not be a man of our lands, stranger, for if you were, you would know that we hold women here in very high esteem," he said in a stern tone, his voice resounding through the hall. He looked over at the queen, who gave him an approving look in return. Turning back to focus his attention on the man he demanded, "What is your name?"

"Noirrash." The man replied loudly, and hung his head in submission, but continued to mumble under his breath. Oslan only caught the words "only a serving girl", and was glad Bowregard seemed not to hear. The king gave the man a warning, telling him that if any of his kingdom's subjects were found injured by any man's hand, he would not only be disqualified from the tournament, but would find himself in the stocks or worse. He continued to address the whole room, encouraging those present to avoid all such situations. He suggested that while they were guests in his kingdom they keep their cool, lest they lose their head.

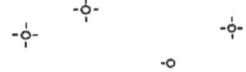

Chapter 18
~ Miles Away ~

Zaltreous hurried smoothly across the university campus, easily managing an armload of heavy leather bound books. His sleek jet black hair was slicked back as usual, without a hair out of place. He looked good, with ice blue eyes, high cheekbones and a strong jaw-line. His clothes were always the latest fashion, and his tailor was a miracle worker. His outfits always fit perfectly, hiding his flaws and bringing out his broad shoulders. Many girls had noticed him, but he only had eyes for one elusive girl. A smile touched his lips as he saw the flame-like hair ahead gleam in the sun and he increased his speed to catch up.

When he reached the two girls who walked and giggled as they talked, he held back so he could listen unnoticed to their conversation. He knew both girls were in his Almatrae language class, but he only cared for the girl on the left, Magdolyn, she of the fiery red hair. The girl on the right, Rebekkah, prattled on about a group of boys she had met at one of the local taverns. Her wavy thickly layered hair moved as she talked animatedly to her friend, sending off waves of a cloying fruity scent. He grimaced when he caught a whiff of it, and moved a few paces to the left, preferring the other girl's intoxicating fragrance. Evidently, Rebekkah was trying to persuade Magdolyn to join her at the Iridescent Iris Inn where she was to meet up with them again. *Ha! Fat chance she has of that,* he thought. He had tried repeatedly to get her to accompany him to that very pub, but though her boyfriend, or rather *fiancée* she had corrected him a number of times to the point of tiring, had been gone for almost four years, she still only had eyes for him. *Lazelan,* he thought sickly, *has he taken every sweet intention from my life?*

The only time Zaltreous had managed to spend alone with her had been as study buddies. He had feigned stupidity in their mutual class to attain her help as a tutor. In reality, he spoke Almatrae fluidly due to his spell-casting classes, in fact he had already taken this very class three years ago, passing with flying colours. It was the language of magic, the ancient high language. There were many a great spell written in Almatrae, many dark ones too, and any mage worth his salt had to speak it fluently to gain any real power. As it turned out, he had an aptitude for magic, and was secretly almost bilingual in the language. Not that he'd ever let on to her. He was not about to lose the one avenue that had brought him success in his plan to woo her for himself. He was brought back to the present by Rebekkah's prattling.

"Seriously, Maggie, just come, it will be fun. You don't have to *date* any of them, just meet them. They're great guys, plus I told them that I would bring a pretty friend next time I came!"

"Bekkah! You know how I feel about gallivanting around. Lazelan would be furious if he knew I was even thinking about going out to a pub to meet a bunch of other guys!" Maggie exclaimed.

"Well luckily, Lazelan isn't here! Besides, he's into doing the right thing and such. How would he feel if he knew you let your best friend walk right into the lion's den without so much as an ally with her for support. I mean come on! Suppose it goes poorly or they don't have enough money to cover my drinks!" Rebekkah pressed.

"Then you pay for what you order." Maggie explained, as if to a five year old.

"Ha!" Rebekkah laughed, "Let's assume for a

moment that I already spent all my pocket money on a new broach in the market."

"Oh, so you not only want me to go to a dark, smelly tavern, but you also do me the honour of insisting that I buy your dinner for you?" Maggie asked teasingly.

"Only if the guys don't pay for it first. Besides, I wasn't going to go for dinner as well, but if you want to throw that in too..." Rebekkah let her voice trail off.

"Oh fine, don't say I never do you any favours. You owe me a big one, and I'll collect on it one day, you can count on that!"

Shocked at this new development, Zaltreous chose that moment to catch up to the two girls. "So you've finally decided to brave the world!" he said cheerfully.

"Not that it's any business of yours!" Rebekkah shot back rudely. "How long were you eves-dropping this time?"

He put a hurt expression on his face. "You do me a great injustice, Rebekkah, I merely caught up to you at a most opportune time."

"I'll just bet you did." She huffed under her breath.

He eyed her warily for a moment, then turned cheerful again, this time addressing Magdolyn. "And just where are you venturing out this fine evening? May I be so lucky to accompany you two fine ladies?"

Rebekkah answered first, "Not this time Zaltreous, we're having a girls' night out!"

"But wouldn't you prefer to have a gentleman with you, especially on the long walk home in case some rowdy drunk person won't take no for an answer?" he asked smoothly. "Besides, I am in desperate need of some tutoring before our exam next week, and we could depart together after that."

At the mention of rowdy drunken men in the street, Magdolyn started noticeably. "Perhaps it isn't such a good idea for us to go alone after all. I know you want me to come, Bekkah, but if something were to happen..." she let the phrase hang in the air, not wanting to mention all the possibilities that might occur for two young ladies out alone at night.

"Oh fine!" Rebekkah all but growled, "You've managed to weasel your way into our plans again, Zaltreous."

"Oh Bekkah, do at least try to be nice. Zaltreous is my friend." Magdolyn urged.

Friend, Zaltreous spat in his mind. *One day I'll be so much more.*

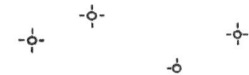

Chapter 19
~ Flummoxed ~

After the grand meal, the tournament goers and participants alike filed out into the evening with full bellies to watch Lazelan's long awaited sky explosion display. The cool evening air carried on it scents of wood shavings from the newly built stands. They took their seats around the gaming arena that had been erected for the event. It was much like the knights' training arena, but outdoors and about five times the size. There were more seats, more battle space, and this arena even had a built in platform centred in the middle of one side with a canopy for honoured guests to accompany the royalty that would sit on magnificently carved wooden thrones. The seats were full by the time the men, boys and knights that were to compete entered the battle arena.

Aylan recognized Carn, Ormond, Thorn, Bow, and joining them all, Oslan himself decked head to toe in newly polished armour. She turned as Millie bustled up, joining her. Aylan pointed out Bow to her, and heard his dad say "Has Thornton not yet given up that gigantic bow?" This was followed by a rustle of clothing as Bow's mother elbowed him to remind him that they shared mixed company. Aylan smiled to herself. The sky was casting oranges, reds, pinks and yellows as the sun bade its last farewell before sinking below the tree-line far off in the distance.

It's almost time. Aylan thought excitedly. Once the sun slipped away, it would be time for Lazelan's show. She would help silently from the stands as her powers, like Sasha, were still a secret to the kingdom. In fact, most of the common folk that were here tonight would go home in awe.

Lazelan's presence and abilities in the kingdom were renowned; however, most commoners had never seen magic first hand. Herbologists were more common, but the art of herbology was seen as something akin to doctoring, less mystic and more helpful for the most part.

Tonight's show would be a mixture of herbology and magic. Lazelan and Aylan had picked the right plants, dug up minerals and shaved metals then prepared them into mixtures that would cause fire to change different colours. He had gone beyond herbology, teaching her how including different metal filaments would produce colours in the flames that the herbs wouldn't. The knights would even take part in the grand finale.

To start the show, Lazelan would throw some pouches into the air and the two mages would use magic to make them fly higher to keep the people watching out of danger of falling fiery bits. Then Aylan would help cause them to explode into flames from the stands. The contents would make the flames burn different colours. The knights had been given pouches of each mixture and stood in a line in a certain order. They were to throw them straight up into the air all at once on cue from Lazelan. It would take both Lazelan and Aylan working together to carry the pouches into the sky to a safe distance, where they would both send out a blast of magic, igniting the flames all at once. Lazelan and Aylan had practised moving certain colours around together. When the colour of each pouch's flame became apparent, they would be moved into position so that they would make an image of a dragon's head blasting fire like on the kingdom's insignia. It was going to be magnificent.

The king stood to address the crowd. A hush fell over the onlookers as they waited attentively for

Eurilas to speak.

"My beloved citizens of Endalwynndale, exceptional guests from afar and honourable knights, welcome to my lands and tournament. Many worthy men have come to prove their mettle, but not one of you knows what is truly at stake." He raised his voice and motioned with his right hand to the far side of the arena. The gate at one end opened and in walked a stable boy dressed in the castle's livery, leading a brilliant black stallion. Behind him, a smaller boy entered. The younger, clearly his brother from their matching brown hair and eyes, leading a well groomed dog.

The king waited until they had taken their places in front of his dais and continued. "You gentlemen will be competing for these; the third place winner will be given this purebred, trained hunting dog. The second place winner will be awarded this splendid black stallion, riding saddle and bridal. And the first place winner will be awarded land in my kingdom." A gasp and excited murmuring filled the arena from the crowd. Many of the competitors' faces brightened with surprised joy. But the king wasn't done yet. "If any competitor wins his event and is not yet a knight, they will be knighted, and will be honoured with their own coat of arms. Lastly, if a man already knighted wins, he will be granted a new suit of armour bearing my kingdom's insignia."

A cheer went up through the crowd. At first, it was seemingly random shouts of appreciation and clapping, but after a few moments, it broke into a few voices shouting "Long live King Eurilas, long live the king!" over and over. After three or four of these calls, the whole crowd began to echo it. Before long, the sound could be heard throughout the arena, grounds, and palace.

The king returned to his plush velvety throne, and Lazelan stepped forward. It was time for the sky-fire show. He held up his hands to quiet the crowd. "What you're about to see may bewilder or frighten you. I assure you, it is all planned, organized and safe. You may see things here tonight that you have only dreamed of, all I ask is that you sit back and enjoy."

*   *   *

Zaltreous closed his door. It was one of many wooden doors down a corridor in the dormitory where the students all lived during their time at the university. He went to his sleeping cot and pulled an elegant mirror out from under the mattress. He had stolen it in the marketplace earlier that year and it was one of his prized possessions. It was a lady's hand-held mirror with a silver frame of embossed roses that surrounded the oval looking glass. The roses went all the way around it, with stems that became the handle. The back was smooth, and felt cool to the touch. He couldn't care less about the beauty of the mirror, he loved it only for its purpose. He waved a hand in front of the glass, saying an incantation in perfect Almatrae, and the mirror stopped reflecting. For a split second, the mirror's surface seemed to shimmer, and then the reflection of his face was replaced with a scene from very far away:

A couple of guards brought a horse's drinking trough into the tournament arena, followed by a succession of boys carrying buckets of water. The trough was placed in front of a platform, and standing on the platform was Lazelan. Zaltreous was unaware that he began to frown in disgust as he watched. Each boy poured his bucketful into the trough until it was filled. Lazelan produced five packets to start. He threw them up, and carried them the rest of the way with magic. All of a sudden, they burst into an explosion of bright flames.

Zaltreous dropped the mirror in surprised and it clattered face down to the floor. He dove for the mirror and snatched it up, hoping against hope that it was not shattered. He picked it up, and his heart seemed to skip a beat when he realized it was still intact. He hugged it to his chest briefly as he let out a sigh of relief. He would have to recast another scrying spell though. He had been startled into dropping the mirror and had lost his concentration on the first spell, forfeiting it. He said the incantation again and waved his hand to bring back the picture. This time he watched for a while as the little packets exploded. He wasn't frightened this time, and sat seething as his loathing grew toward the man producing the show.

Cheap parlour tricks. Why does he waste his time? Zaltreous wondered as he watched. *He has so much more power than this, and a talent for it that nearly comes close to mine. Why doesn't he put it to real use? He could own that kingdom and yet there he sits, entertaining the king and his nobles. He's nothing more than a glorified jester! He doesn't deserve her, I would give her the whole kingdom.*

Then, just for fun, because the mood so struck him, he began casting another spell. A less powerful mage would only be able to scry, however, Zaltreous had studied secretly for years. His abilities were quite formidable. Not only could he scry, but he was so powerful that with the right spells, he could affect the things he saw through the glass. He watched the next group of packets soar up into the air and burst into flames of different colours. They moved into formation to form a dragon's head blowing fire. It was really quite impressive, until Zaltreous made it more so. He pointed his fingertips at the mirror's image and said another incantation.

*   *   *

Suddenly, in Endalwynndale, the flaming dragon made of packets in the sky seemed to move slightly. The few making up the left eye shifted and made the dragon seem as though it was winking. Lazelan was baffled at this new turn of events. He wasn't prepared for it and his concentration started to slip. He looked over to Aylan and saw on her face pure shock as well. Packets started to tumble out of the sky, but as they fell over the arena, they swerved and moved and started tumbling downward toward the onlookers. People started to shift in their places uneasily as flaming sacks letting off acrid fumes were hurled toward their upturned faces.

Aylan thought quickly, and harnessed the lowest packets with her mind. She sent out a wave of energy that forced them off their course. She steered them toward the horse's trough. With a mighty succession of splashes, the sacs dove into the water where they were extinguished with a hot sizzle and bout of steam. Lazelan followed her lead and they managed to catch every packet before anyone was hurt. Each one found its way safely into the water. When the last one hit, the trough was almost dry, only a soggy pile of sizzling packets were left. There was startled silence from the crowd and then the place erupted in a deafening cheer. People laughed, yelled, clapped and stomped in enjoyment of such a wondrous display.

*   *   *

Back in his room, disgusted, Zaltreous ended his spells and replaced the mirror under his mattress.

Chapter 20
~ I Scry With My Little Eye ~

Aylan, Sasha, Oslan and Lazelan were in his laboratory discussing the events of the evening. The festivities had ended for the night, folks had retired to the bars and inns to either continue to celebrate late into the night, or get rested for the tournament's first event the next day.

During the sky-fire display, Lazelan and Aylan had both seen their packet dragon wink. They told Oslan that as they had struggled to hold the flaming sachets in the sky, they had both felt a force working against them.

"I'm both glad and disturbed to hear it," confided the prince, "I am relieved that it wasn't your doing to bring the packets so close to our guests. I must admit, I was a little nervous that someone might get hurt. At the same time, I wondered what could have caused it."

"Your people almost did get hurt, Sire. Aylan and I had our hands full trying to keep the packets from raining down onto the crowded stands. They were definitely being forced that way. Someone may have been watching without being there," Lazelan confided. "But that is what upsets me; it means that a powerful mage might wish us harm."

Lazelan tried to explain that most young mages were capable of feats that would strike non-magic folk as awe-inspiring. Simply scrying, the act of using a smooth surface to see people and places far away, would seem incredible to a commoner. However, a mage's powers were limited not only by the incantations they knew and their ability to manipulate the world around them, but also by the amount of energy he or she possessed. He explained to the prince that a mage's powers grew as they practiced, just as a knight's muscles were strengthened by using bigger and heavier swords as Oslan did for training.

Usually, it took years for a mage to have the energy needed to do anything considered really impressive. If one were to try to cast a spell that would drain too much of his or her energy, one of two things could happen. The first was that the one who cast the spell could draw from another mage's source if they joined their concentration and energy together to aid one another.

The other alternative was very bad. The mage could use up all of their energy pool. If this happened, and the spell was not yet complete, it would draw from the only energy source left: the mage's life force. If this too was drained by the spell, the mage might die. If the effort did not kill the mage, yet their energy pool was used up, they may not be able to replenish it, and would lose the ability to cast spells in the future. That part of them might be dead to them forever.

"What makes you think that it was a powerful mage working against us?" Aylan asked.

Instead of answering right away, Lazelan posed a question to Oslan: "Are there any other folk with magic that you know of in the kingdom?"

"Not amongst its citizens, however, there are so many strangers from far off lands here for the tournament, it could be possible." Oslan replied.

"We need to find out, for I fear the worst." Lazelan urged. Then, answering Aylan's question, he continued, "It took two of us to hold and move the packets the way we wanted in the sky for the show."

"So we wouldn't drain our energy pools," Aylan interjected.

"Yes," Lazelan continued, smiling at his apt

pupil. "But whoever was working against us was forcing the packets down, not just letting them fall. Someone was directing them in order to cause damage. That in itself would take a lot of energy. I suspect however, that it wasn't an onlooker that was present."

"What makes you say that?" the prince asked.

Sasha spoke up at this point "I would have seen it, your majesty. I scanned the crowd, and had no visions or premonitions of anything amiss with any of our guests. That must mean that whoever was to blame was too far away from the event for my gift of sight to reach them."

The prince digested this information. "So Lazelan, tell me, how does one cast magic on us when they aren't even there?"

"Perhaps in one's sleep?" enquired Aylan, remembering the first time she used magic. "They wouldn't be within Sasha's immediate sight, but they could have been close by."

Lazelan shook his head slowly, "No, I'm afraid that this situation called for magic that was precise, since we were moving the packets, and it was keeping up. To work against us in such a fashion would take great skill. In a dream, someone *might* be able to influence the packets, but not on such a grand scale, and not with the constant changes caused by our interference. I fear someone was watching from afar. I believe it was someone using a scrying spell, Your Majesty. I believe that they not only held the spell, but also cast more magic through the object they were using to scry. That kind of magic is incredibly difficult, and would take a tremendous amount of power. Most mages wouldn't even attempt it alone."

There was silence in the room as the four pondered this. "My kingdom has been peaceful for years," said the prince sadly, "who would wish us harm? And to what end? I must discuss this with my father and his general. Thank you for your expertise, Lazelan." With that, the prince withdrew and returned through the secret passage to the war room and the palace halls beyond.

"As for myself," Sasha announced, "I will return to my chambers to put myself into a trance. Perhaps I will be able to see the offender or their next trick so we can be ready for it." Sasha quitted the room, leaving Aylan and Lazelan alone to talk of magic.

Intrigued, she begged him to show her how to scry, but he flatly refused. He told her that although she was showing an amazing aptitude for magic, and she had proven that her powers were growing, the energy they had expended keeping the crowd safe was too much. He promised to teach her the next morning, and that she should head to bed as he wouldn't train her again until she was well rested.

*   *   *

The next morning, Lazelan met Aylan in the early hours before the tournament was to start, and knights still slumbered in their beds. She sat now at his wooden worktable, her chipped water basin in front of her filled halfway with clear cool water. As usual, candles burned near the walls to give them a dim yellow glowing light to work by. Aylan placed her hands upon the table's surface, feeling the dry wood's grain and round knots. "Say the incantation, and send your energy onto the water. It helps if you focus it through your hand, and pass it over the water's surface." Lazelan guided.

Aylan thought about what she might like to see. She pondered looking in on the prince, but decided not to in case she might see things that were meant for private eyes, like a council meeting or worse. She decided upon searching for a place as opposed to a person. "What is the name of your land, Lazelan?" she enquired.

"It is called Ethik." He answered with approval.

"Vearta uta da Ey seche ot isa. Vearta Ethik" *Reveal that which I seek to see. Reveal Ethik,* She thought. As she spoke the words in the mystic ancient language, she focused her inner power and passed her hand over the gleaming water's surface. The reflection it gave of the candles nearby flickered, swirled, and faded. It was replaced by a picture of green grasslands, short stone buildings and sunlight. "Your land is beautiful." Aylan mused as she stared in awe as two children not much younger than she appeared at the edge of the reflection. They were running through the grass, the girl holding an orange orb in her hand that was flecked with black. "What is that thing that the girl has?" Aylan asked.

Lazelan leaned over the basin to see what Aylan was seeing. He laughed at the sight. "It's an orange, much like the ones from around here, but smaller. In the towns around my part of the kingdom, this is a tradition. People will push herbs called cloves into the orange, then offer it to another to remove with their teeth. It's sort of a kind of game."

When Aylan looked back down into the basin of water, she discovered that it once again reflected only the flickering candles on the table next to it.

"What happened to Ethik?" she asked.

Lazelan chuckled. "You broke your concentration on your spell. You looked up at me and in listening to me yammer on about oranges and cloves, you forgot about what you were doing. You're going to have to recast it."

Aylan made to move her hand over the water once more but Lazelan gently but firmly told her she would have to wait until later to try it again, lest she burn herself out. "Ethik is a long way away, and your magic had to reach all the way there to bring us the picture. You need your rest," he cautioned. She contented herself with learning more about the orange game from Lazelan's land instead. She sat with him, and asked many questions, starting with how to make the cloves stick to the sweet fruit. Meanwhile, the castle was beginning to wake for the tournament in the rooms all around them.

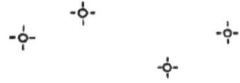

Chapter 21
~ Clove n' Hooves ~

Lazelan and Aylan had left the workshop not long after that to attend to things for later in the day. Separating in the courtyard, Lazelan continued on to the arena and Aylan travelled to the kitchen for an orange. Once that had been procured, she collected Millie from her room and they went on a hike in the king's forest to find cloves. Although Oslan was to compete later in the afternoon, when he caught the two girls trying to sneak away, he insisted on accompanying them for their own protection. On top of that, he insisted that they take horses to speed their journey along so as not to be too late to ready himself for the competition.

"We should really have Carn with us too," He grumbled as the horses' hooves made soft thumps on the forest's soil, "What if we get approached by something bigger than an imp? What are you searching for cloves for anyway, aren't there enough spices in Lazelan's laboratory for you to take your pick?"

"Then you will smash the bigger-than-an-imp thing with your mighty sword and it will be good practice for later!" Aylan shot in before Millie could answer him about the cloves. She didn't want to tell the prince about it until it was all prepared and she surprised him with the first round of the game. They hiked for a half hour before they came to the spot where cloves could be picked. They managed to gather enough to satisfy Aylan, and with her back to Oslan, she set about using magic to dry out the cloves so they would be palatable. She placed her hands on either side of her small harvest, and said her incantation: "Umek wahss est taek, wornd utae grechae." *With heat and air, dry these herbs.*

Suddenly, a wave of warm dry wind seemed to come together between her hands, tossing the cloves around slightly as the magic worked. After a few moments, she let the magic collapse and she picked up a clove to examine her handy work.

Satisfied with what she had done, she gingerly bit into one of the cloves. The strong taste flooded her mouth, making her saliva glands tickle and shoot saliva into her mouth. She spat out the clove and proceeded to poke the remaining cloves into the orange, pointy end first. When she was done, the orange looked like it was covered in brown buds. With a blooming smile, she finally turned to the prince and offered him the orange.

The prince's face showed a quick expression of happy familiarity, and surprisingly, he winked at her. Aylan was shocked, and stood frozen with the orange held out between them. Unruffled, Oslan glanced at Millie, then bent his head over the orange long enough to pull a clove out with his teeth, and then looked up to grin at Aylan. Aylan stood looking at the clove poking out from between his teeth, and didn't move.

They stood facing each other for a moment, neither of them moving. "I don't think Lazelan taught you to play this right." He announced. He took the orange and held it out to Aylan the same way she had offered it to him. She bent over the orange, reaching up to steady it with her hands. She was conscious of her fingertips brushing his hand and felt her heart beat just a little faster as she pulled out a clove with her teeth. The taste of cloves still lingered on her tongue from before, but now it was joined by a slight hint of orange juice. She took the clove from her mouth and threw it away, grinning. Lowering the orange, Oslan stepped closer to Aylan than he'd ever been before. She could smell the leather and sweat on him and for a moment she felt giddy, right up until he slowly leaned in and gently kissed her on the cheek.

Aylan gasped, and her hand shot up to her face, where it was rewarded by the warm touch of her skin. She was blushing. *Oh great, I'll never live this down! What was he thinking anyway? Not that I might not offer him the orange again...*she thought. What she said though was a muttled jumble of consonants and vowels that could only be described as sputtering. She finally managed an incensed "You *kissed* me!" Millie stood to the side, looking from one shocked face to the other, her rosy lips slowly beginning to spread into an incredulous smile.

"Only your cheek, and besides, you asked me to!" the prince protested, looking worried. Then his face cleared and he started bellowing with laughter. "Boy, Lazelan sure didn't explain it to you well at all!" As Aylan stood watching, dumbfounded, Oslan continued while doubling over. "Aylan, depending on how the recipient removes the clove, the person with the orange will receive a different kind of kiss. The orange clove is a kissing game!"

"And what if I had kept it between my teeth as you did?" she demanded.

Now it was the prince's turn to blush as he answered, "I would have kissed your lips of course." At this, Millie's face burst into a wider grin and grabbing the orange out of the prince's grasp, she raced back to her horse and back down the path toward the tournament. "Wait for us! Where are you going?" Aylan yelled as she mounted her horse to pursue her.

Millie flung her answer back over her shoulder as her horse galloped away. It was a single word: "Bowregard!"

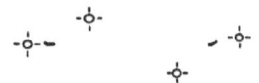

Chapter 22
~ Bar-Fly-on-the-Wall ~

"Tay postikmai kalai vila ert." Zaltreous said confidently as he gazed deeply into Maggie's eyes. She shifted uncomfortably on the couch, then got up and walked away to put some distance between them. She feigned needing a drink so his feelings wouldn't be hurt. He seemed so harmless when he had first come to her asking for help studying. But lately, sometimes she could swear he was trying to make a move on her, an unwelcomed move.

"I believe what you meant was: Tay postikii kalai vila ertae." *You have beautiful green eyes.* "You put the verb in the past tense, and unless I suddenly became a Cyclops, I still have two eyes." She joked to lighten the mood.

Zaltreous plastered a disappointed look on his face. "I really thought I had it that time. I've been practicing all week." He confided.

"Look," she encouraged, feeling slightly sorry for him, "maybe you should just stick with the assignment we're working on in class."

He sighed. "I guess I have been getting better at that, thanks to your help. When you're right, you're right. I'll stick with our class work from now on."

At that point there was a knock at the door. Magdolyn crossed the room to open it, revealing an impatient Rebekkah on the other side. "Come *on*!" she stressed, "You're not even ready yet?"

"We were just about to start working on our school project!" Zaltreous pointed out, angered that his time with Magdolyn had been shortened.

"It will have to wait," Rebekkah declared, "I'm hungry, and Maggie offered to buy me dinner."

Zaltreous gave Rebekkah a withering look,

but allowed his face to brighten as he turned to Magdolyn. "Well if you are treating Rebekkah, then I will treat you."

"That's really not necessary." Magdolyn replied. "I'll just go put my hair up." Magdolyn rushed to fetch her hair combs. She pulled her hair back, held the ringlets in place with the combs, and presented herself to Rebekkah. "Are they in straight?"

Rebekkah rolled her dark eyes and grabbed her hand, pulling her through the still opened door. "Yes, you look fine, you always look perfect." For once, Zaltreous had to agree with her. He had believed that Magdolyn was perfection personified, from the first time Lazelan had introduced them.

The three walked the cobbled streets to the tavern making light conversation about classes, their teachers, and the boys Rebekkah was hoping to meet at the bar. They arrived by and by, and entered to the jovial sound of a bard's tune and many merry makers attempting to sing along...poorly. To raucous applause and cheering, the bard finished his song. He motioned to some other lads with instruments of various kinds, and they joined him in the corner where he played. He continued to strum his lute and the others joined in with a pan flute, a recorder, a Jew's harp, and a mandore. The five began an upbeat tune about a roving man, and Magdolyn and Zaltreous found a table to sit at. Rebekkah checked the faces of the rowdy crowd to see if she recognized anyone, and finally sat in defeat at the table with her friends.

Zaltreous caught a serving wench's attention and demanded some mead, and three suppers. The girl returned quickly with three mugs, expertly weaving her way through the crowd back to their table. She arrived safely, but got jostled by someone in the crowd as she was setting down the mugs, causing some of the mead to slosh onto Magdolyn's wrist. The serving girl acted quickly, grabbing for the cloth at her waist, "Oh! My apologies, Milady. Let me wipe that ri-"

"I'll get that!" Zaltreous interrupted, as he whipped the cloth out of her grasp with his right hand, and took a startled Magdolyn's wet wrist with his left. As he held Magdolyn's hand with a little too much familiarity, he dabbed at her wrist with the cloth, finally returning it to the serving wench as Magdolyn retrieved her hand from his clasp. "Um thanks," she muttered, slightly unnerved.

"Wow, that was creepy," Rebekkah judged, glaring at Zaltreous.

"Isn't that one of the boys you've been searching for all night?" Zaltreous shot back at her, nodding his head in the general direction of the door. Rebekkah glanced over even though she knew he was just trying to mock her, just in case. Her countenance brightened as she realized that it was in fact one of her sought after gentlemen. She immediately got up to rush over to him, but stopped, glancing at Magdolyn to see if she was ok to be left alone. After an encouraging "Go on!" from Maggie, Rebekkah skipped away across the room to meet her friend.

Finally alone! Zaltreous thought. He seized the opportunity to start up a conversation to break Magdolyn's unwavering faith in Lazelan. "You must miss Lazelan terribly," He started, always as the understanding friend.

"You know I do," Magdolyn replied, "but it shan't be too long now, he has had great success with his student, and shall be returning soon!"

Zaltreous started at this news. He hadn't known that Lazelan had even found a student.

"Oh?" he asked very casually, hoping for more information that could help him.

"Her name is Aylan," Magdolyn informed him, "and apparently she is a prodigy. Soon she'll be ready to take over his position and he will be heading home to marry me."

I can't let that happen. He thought in alarm, *I'm not ready for him to come back yet.* "Is she pretty?" Zaltreous asked, planting a seed of doubt in her mind.

"I wouldn't know," She replied indignantly, "it doesn't really matter, he loves me. Besides, she sounds like little more than a child."

"So you're not worried that he may think of her...fondly?" he pursued.

"Not at all. When it comes to Lazelan, I don't worry," she said persuasively, although her confidence looked shaken.

"You know," Zaltreous ventured, "I would never have left you in the first place."

"That's because you weren't offered the job, they gave it to Lazelan instead!" Rebekkah said from behind him. "Come on, Maggie, let's go see why our food hasn't come yet." Magdolyn glanced at her gratefully as she rose and the girls left the table in search of their serving wench.

"Tough break, my friend." Rebekkah's blond beau commented as he sat down at the table with Zaltreous. "What does that guy have that you don't have?" he asked in male comradery. "Money? Power? Connections?"

"Aside from her undying love? All of the above." Zaltreous sighed moodily.

"Too bad you weren't born a king." He commiserated, "They can pretty much have whomever they want."

Not born a king, no, Zaltreous mused,

however, being born into a royal family isn't the only way to become a king. "Let me buy you a drink, my friend," Zaltreous offered as he clapped the other man on the back. "When you're right, you're right."

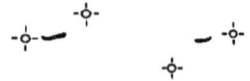

Chapter 23
~ A Vision of Perfection ~

Lazelan and Zaltreous had been friends since their first year at the university. They had shared a couple of classes, and both had been studying to become mages. Though a lot of the outside world thought that mage work was a fabrication and that there was no real future in it, the boys had pursued it for different reasons. Lazelan had like the challenge it offered and the fact that the coursework was so different from other careers that the university trained people for. Zaltreous liked it due to the sheer power it afforded. The boys had shown great potential as they both excelled in their classes, and they became fast friends.

Partway through their first year, as they began to move from being acquaintances to having a real friendship, they decided to go to the tavern just off of campus. It went well, so they made it a regular thing over their next three years there. When they visited the taverns together, they would take turns chatting up the girls from the university that caught their attention. On one such occasion, Zaltreous had just excused himself to go dance with one of the girls he had bought a drink for. Lazelan was left at the bar to order himself another mug of ale. It was then that she appeared. As Zaltreous danced, pre-occupied with the girl in his arms, in walked a red-haired beauty and a pretty brunette.

Lazelan was watching the door as he sipped some ale, and felt the blow of love's first arrow as she entered the tavern. He introduced himself to the girls as they arrived at the bar, and offered them the two seats beside him. He took care of both of their drinks, and introduced himself. After finding out that they had just begun going to the university, they fell into easy conversation while he marvelled at his luck at meeting such a witty, beautiful and clearly intelligent girl. He found her friend to be nice too, but she was clearly scoping out the tavern for her own companion to talk to.

From his place on the dance floor, Zaltreous casually glanced over and saw the astonishing beauty of the girl talking to his friend. He immediately wanted her for himself. She was tall, and had red ringlets that fell in tight curls past her shoulders. She had the straightest, finest nose he'd ever seen, and her wide green eyes seemed to sparkle. He manufactured an excuse in his head that would allow him to leave the girl on the dance floor and rejoin his friend.

Lazelan had hung on every word the red-head said, and by the time Zaltreous had pried himself away from the girl he had met that night, Lazelan was able to introduce the two girls as Rebekkah and Magdolyn. When Zaltreous had walked up, he could see that the two were sitting rather close together, and that the red-headed girl had placed her hand on Lazelan's arm as she laughed at something he said. Not a good sign. Well, not a good sign for Zaltreous. He and Lazelan had never had an argument over a female, yet Zaltreous was adamant that this girl be his. He opened with a smooth pick up line, although Lazelan was clearly interested in the girl too.

Oh well, Zaltreous thought, *he'll just have to get over it.* "Do you have a quill?" he began.

"Excuse me?" Magdolyn asked.

"I asked if you have a quill," Zaltreous continued smoothly, "You see, my mother asked me to write home to her the minute I met the girl of my dreams."

Lazelan glared at Zaltreous, but that look changed to one of incredulity while his heart felt a pang of jealousy. Magdolyn had just laughed and seemingly charmed, she had stepped toward Zaltreous to give him a lush kiss.

*   *   *

Sasha flipped fitfully on her low bed as she dreamed her insightful dreams. She had begun mumbling in her sleep. She was still dreaming about the tavern. In her dream, Lazelan stepped forward, shouting "No!" as Magdolyn and Zaltreous left the bar arm in arm to enter the cold night. In her room, Sasha's "No!" resounded just before she rolled again. Clearing the edge of her bed, she began falling through the short space to the floor. She awoke with a start on impact. She found that the tears that had been on Lazelan's cheeks in the dream were now on her own. It was a warning.

Her dreams had been changing as of late. The ones she had been having for months about Lazelan's upcoming wedding had turned sinister. Instead of the guests being happy and the bride smiling, there were tears coursing down her pretty face. More importantly, Lazelan was not the groom. There was a mysterious pale man with jet black hair in what should have been his place. And now, there was this new dream about their meeting in the tavern.

She had not yet told Lazelan of the dreams about his wedding, but now, with this new figure in more of her dreams, she feared Lazelan's future might be at risk, for how else would his love be willing to wed another? This new tavern dream had given her some ammunition though. Through the introductions in her dream, she now had a name to go with the pale handsome face. Her mind was reeling with the implications of what these dreams could mean. She was fretting too much to sleep, so she sat up cross-legged and forced herself to relax.

She was not done finding information quite yet. She closed her eyes and began counting herself backwards into a trance. She took herself back to the fireworks display. She found, though that she was not watching it from the same vantage point that she had when she had watched the show. She seemed to be watching it from a height, and through some sort of glass. In her trance, she could hear mumbling, a quick silky voice speaking a language she didn't recognize. She watched as the flaming packets made the dragon wink and heard the voice chuckle. Then she heard the words speed up, becoming more insistent. Then she watched as the packets flew from their place in the sky. They weren't all aimed at random peasants she saw. Most of the time, the glass focused on Lazelan. More than one packet headed straight for him for a few moments until it was redirected to the trough of water. The owner of the voice began speaking feverishly in the unknown language, while pausing now and again to curse in the common language. Finally, the picture fogged away as if someone had blown hot breath on a cold window. In its place the face of the boy from the tavern and newer dreams of Magdolyn's wedding swam into view.

Sasha began to bring herself out of her trance. As she counted back from five, her awareness of her own room became more and more lucid until she was fully conscious again. She rose from her bed and dressed in a hurry. The sun had risen just enough to show her that she could still meet Lazelan and Aylan before the day's events.

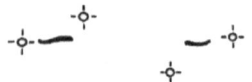

Chapter 24
~ Birds of a Feather ~

When Sasha got to Lazelan's warm laboratory, she was surprised to see that Aylan wasn't there working away in the glow of the flickering candlelight. "The prince has taken her to introduce her to Archer." Lazelan told her.

They exchanged a knowing glance. The prince had never before divulged his secret weapon to a girl. People sometimes wondered at his prowess as a hunter. He almost always came home with something, and though a lot of his game was smaller birds, he succeeded where others had failed. His secret was that he often had a little help. Sasha only knew because one of his hunting trips had shown up in a vision. Lazelan knew because he had been on a trip with Oslan, betting skill against magic to see who could catch the most. The kitchen had been well stocked that night, and there had been a feast to celebrate.

"I think the prince quite fancies her." Sasha commented.

"Yes, but I'm not sure he even realizes it yet," Lazelan mused. "In any case, he'd never admit it. He's going to have to marry soon, and I'm not sure the king would approve of a common girl, skilled in magic or not."

"Oh, his heart will break," lamented Sasha.

"Which is why he won't admit his feelings, even to himself," Lazelan pressed.

They left such topics then and Sasha told Lazelan about her visions. As she talked, his brow furrowed, his skin paled, and he needed to sit down.

"You described almost perfectly the night we met," he informed her, except the kiss and them leaving together, that is. In reality, she left with me.

What does it mean?"

"Perhaps the prince isn't the only man afflicted with feelings for a lady," she pondered.

"He would never touch Maggie. We've been best friends for years and he knows what she means to me. It must have just been a dream, Sasha." He reasoned in denial.

Sasha shook her head sadly as she took his hands in hers. "Make no mistake, I also found out that he is the one that sabotaged your fire display at the tournament." She added sadly.

"But why would he do it Sasha? The packets weren't attacking me, it was an attack on the audience. What purpose would that serve him?" he asked.

"Perhaps he means to discredit you. If the townsfolk were to be harmed, you may have been to blame for the incident. The king knew you were the one controlling the packets. You might have been outcast or worse, put to death for endangering the king."

Lazelan pondered this last thought for a long while before continuing, "If I had been banished, I would have returned to Maggie and married her. How would that help him?"

"If you had been dismissed and returned home, you would have done so without training an apprentice." Sasha pointed out, "You would have returned in disgrace. You would not have been able to take your place at the university and you would have no kind of life to offer Magdolyn." Then she added gently: "Are you sure her parents would still have allowed her to wed you?"

Lazelan's countenance turned grim. "Aylan is almost ready, I must get home Sasha, to save Maggie and to take my place at her side before my sometime friend can do more damage. If he wants to take me out of the equation, then I am endangering everyone here by staying."

*   *   *

Oslan led Aylan up the curving steps leading to one of the castle's towers. The stairway was enclosed with stone as it wound around and up to the room at the top. Sections of the staircase were warm and darkened between the points that were pierced with light and the fresh breeze afforded by the many arrow slits they passed along the way. At the top of the stairs, there was a heavy wooden door with a thick metal lock. Oslan pulled a necklace out of his shirt, and held up the key that was dangling from it. With a flourish and a grin, he announced importantly: "This is one of the kingdom's prized possessions."

Aylan cocked her head as she regarded the prince for a moment. One side of her pretty mouth pulled up into a slanting smile. She blinked once, slowly, and twisted the fingers on her right hand. "Sauxel," *unlock.* The prince started as he heard an audible click from behind him. He tried the handle and frowned as the door easily slid open. "I'll have to talk to Lazelan about this one," he grimaced. He stood aside and allowed her to enter first, always the gentleman. As she passed him, she thought that she caught the scent of cloves about him. Startled, she smiled to herself as she remembered that same smell mixed with oranges in the forest. Then she entered the room at the top of the tower.

Before her, feathers drifted lazily on the warm air, in and out of the slanted rays of sunlight entering through the windows. There was an underlying odour of fowl and scat that filled the space. In places, the wood floor was slick with it, so

Aylan took care where to step. From the floor, seven wooden stands rose up, each supporting a glorious bird. They ranged in size and colour, but all were predators.

After letting her take in the room, Oslan quietly stepped up beside Aylan and took her hand. It was smooth and warm, and Aylan prayed that her hand would not start to sweat and give away how excited and nervous she was. As their eyes met, he did not drop her hand, but led her toward a sleek looking bird on a middle stand. "These are the mews," explained the prince, "This is where my family keeps some of our most loved treasures." He was about to go on when one let out a magnificent screech as the pair approached.

When they stopped, just out of nipping range of the bird, Oslan turned to face her, still holding her hand. Aylan felt her heart speed up. *Oh my,* she thought, *is this to be the venue of another kiss? I'm not sure how I feel about that with all of these birds staring at us,* her mind reeled. *I mean, he's so handsome,* she finally admitted to herself, *and wonderful, but they're all just...just...watching!* Oslan leaned slowly closer, and Aylan realized that she didn't care if the birds were watching or not. She tilted her face up to his and let her eyes slide closed.

But he surprised her and instead of leaning in for a kiss, he whispered in her ear instead: "Would you mind terribly handing me that glove? You see, it's all the way over there, and you're in my way." As he spoke, her eyes flew open and his flicked to a place over her shoulder. Aylan's mouth started flapping open and closed like a fish out of water.

The prince chuckled, but using her hand, spun her around so she could see the black leather glove hanging on a hook halfway across the room. "Only one thing," he added," I'm not sure that I'm ready to relinquish your hand quite yet." At this Aylan smiled knowingly. He wished to see more of her skills as a mage. *Okay,* she thought*, he wants to see what I can do? Let's start with something simple.* "Fli," *Levitate.* She said the word and raised her empty hand, palm up.

The glove rose several inches, straight up, coming loose of the nail that had supported it moments before. It hung there in the air, not moving. "Flikt ot Ey," *fly to me,* she amended. She motioned her fingers forward and the glove seemed to follow as it flew across the lofty room. Oslan lifted his hand as if to grab it from the air, but Aylan told him not to move as she twisted her fingers, turning the glove in the air. Now the glove would slide neatly onto his outstretched hand.

Why shouldn't I show off a little, she reasoned, *he asked for it.* As if he could read her mind, the prince raised the hand he possessed to his chest, placing it over his heart. She could feel it's beating under the soft black velvet of his doublet that was being crushed by her fingertips. Her own heart sped up, pulse racing. The glove continued to hover in the air, but its course jogged slightly.

He stared deeply into her face and she got lost in his amber eyes. The glove began to falter in the air. He sealed the glove's fate as he leaned in to kiss her. Thinking now only of their soft and warm embrace, Aylan lost control of her spell and the glove made a *flump* sound as it hit the ground at their feet.

As if on cue, the prince finished his kiss, and pulled back, releasing her. He looked down at the glove and nudged it with his toe. "Looks like you've still got a little work to do on holding your concentration." He teased her. Then he sobered, "That is an important skill you must have in the middle of a battle when distractions like flaming arrows are sailing all around you."

Aylan stared in wonder as Oslan picked up and donned the thick black leather glove. She was incensed. She felt used. She was about to raise her voice to him, but he shushed her, warning that if she yelled, she would upset the birds. He told her gently that he wanted to show her someone special, and offered her the hand not in the glove. She made no move to take it, turning her nose up slightly instead. He seemed momentarily distraught, then turned his back to her. He held his gloved arm down in front of the perch and the bird calmly stepped onto his wrist. It settled there comfortably, and regarded her with its golden eyes.

"Aylan, meet Archer," The prince introduced while he kept his back to her. She thought that his voice might have waivered as he stroked the large bird's dark bluish-black head and back. Its throat was white and its chest was flecked with the darkest black-brown. Its wings were the same bluish-black right to the tips, which were solid and dark. It looked majestic perched on Oslan's arm, and it turned its head slowly to keep her in view whenever Oslan moved.

"She is my peregrine falcon, my secret weapon when I hunt. I was thinking of bringing her to today's tournament. She can only be bested by my father's gyr falcon, the large white one on the first stand." He turned to face Aylan while he pointed in the direction of the larger gyr, but let his hand and his head fall when he realized she was no longer there.

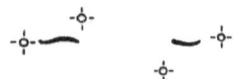

Chapter 25
~ A Secret Favour ~

Aylan returned to the corridor that held her room, seething mad. *How dare he take leave to kiss me!* She raged in her mind. *Practice my concentration indeed! How could he go on about his bird like nothing had happened?* She threw open her door and stormed inside, startling Millie, who was once again letting down the hem of Aylan's tunics. Alarmed at the sight of Aylan, who was red in the face, she set aside her sewing and rushed to Aylan's side, offering her support.

"Tell me what happened!" Millie urged.

"He *kissed* me, that's what happened!" Aylan fumed.

"Who kissed you?" Millie asked, though she thought she already knew.

"Oslan, who else?" Alan griped, "Who else would assume that just because they're royalty, they can go around kissing whomever they like?"

Millie was shocked at this outburst. "I thought you liked the kiss!"

"Of *course* I liked the kiss," Aylan ranted, "That's not the issue. If he's going to kiss me, he should at least mean it!"

"But you offered him the orange first!" Millie protested.

Aylan stopped pacing the room long enough to throw Millie a comical look of confusion. Then understanding dawned on her face. She stopped pacing and sagged down onto her bed. "He kissed me again. Upstairs, not five minutes ago."

She turned to Millie and offered her a seat next to her on the bed. Now it was Millie's turn to look confused. "Then shouldn't you be happy? It's obvious that the prince likes you."

Aylan felt her traitor heart flutter. *Stop that,* she thought, *we're being angry right now!* "He only kissed me as a test. He wanted to see some magic, so I showed off a little," she admitted glumly. "He kissed me to try to break my concentration. It worked, I lost the spell."

"So what are you really upset about? The fact that he kissed you, or the fact that your spell failed?" Millie challenged her.

"I suppose I'm upset because maybe I wish that Oslan would *want* to kiss me," she confessed.

"But he's kissed you twice," Millie pointed out.

"Yes, but always for a game or a scheme, never yet because he simply wanted to," Aylan insisted.

Millie leaned in to talk in a low conspiratorial voice. "I have it under good authority that His Royal Highness is crazy about you," Millie declared.

Aylan's heart skipped a beat. *Argh, stop that!* "And under whose authority might that be?" she asked warily, not wanting to believe without any proof.

"Well," Millie gushed, "When I took that orange from you to the boys' barracks to find Bow, I caught the boys talking about it. Apparently, Oslan speaks in high regard of you. Something happened in the arena after the sky-fire show. The prince arrived late to the arena, and came in as one of the boys, Aloysius, sort of poked fun at your expense because he had noticed you in the crowd dressed as a boy. Oslan overheard it. He vaulted the wall of the arena, landing in front of the startled boy. Thornton said that he's never seen anyone move that fast. Oslan told Aloysius that one of the jobs of the king's knights was to act honorably and protect those that could not protect themselves. He pointedly told the boy that while you were not here you were unable to defend yourself. He went on to tell him that you were to be considered under his protection. He also told Aloysius that if he talked in a dishonorable manor about any lady again, that Oslan would make sure personally that the boy would never receive his fire."

Aylan sat with her mouth agape and her heart soaring. *Alright, you win, flutter away.* "I have to go find him and make things right."

"Sasha might have already taken care of that for you," Millie said guiltily.

"What do you mean?" asked Aylan quickly, "What has she done?"

"Well, she came in just before you did, all in a thither. She was all flushed and anxious, spouting that if someone didn't act fast, that history as we will know it one day might change!" Millie reported. "She asked me for a swatch of cloth or some such thing of yours, but I told her that I wasn't allowed to go through your things. She rummaged in your trunk and came out with a length of turquoise fabric. She cried: "That's it!" Then, she rushed out as quickly as she had come."

Aylan's eyes widened and her mouth formed an almost perfect round O. Without another word, she raced from the room, now needing to find Oslan and Sasha both. She ran back to the tower which housed the mews, taking the stairs two at a time. She flung her spell, "Sauxel," *unlock,* at the door when she was still five steps away, turning her fingers in front of her as she ran. Gaining the top step, she collided with the door as it held fast. Her body recoiled from the percussion, causing her to almost lose her footing. She fell back three stairs while a sharp pain raced up the arm she had held out to push open the door. She climbed the last stairs again and frantically tried the latch with the other hand, but it would not budge. It took her a moment to realize that her spell had not worked. Once again, she had not concentrated hard enough on the task at hand.

She took a deep breath, cleared her mind as best she could, and tried to recast her spell. "Sauxel," *unlock*, she repeated in a much calmer state. Her fingers twisted, the pain in her wrist flared, but this time the door mercifully unlocked. She flung open the door and entered the aviary, startling the falcons on their perches. She focused on the centre stand and saw Oslan's great bird was missing. She departed again, relocking the door behind her as she left with another spell, "El," *lock*.

She travelled as fast as she could on foot down the stairs, through the courtyard, all the way to the outdoor arena where the tournament was taking place. She found Oslan on his horse across the way in the middle of a fray. His falcon was perched on his arm. Many men were battling in the arena all around him. She could tell by their armour and weapons that these were all knights from one place or another, with the exception of Oslan, the prince.

There seemed to be no rhyme or rule to their attacks. They simply tried to take out the closest knight, and then they moved on to the next that was still standing. Squires and other knights-in-training risked many a blow to run into the arena to remove downed knights that lay motionless on the ground. Oslan was not doing well. He looked unfocused, and was barely dodging blows. In fact, to Aylan's eye, he seemed as though he wasn't trying very hard to be missed. *Why isn't he fighting?* She thought frantically.

She could see King Eurilas on his pedestal, wringing his hands in worry over his only son's welfare. Thankfully, the knights that fought for him were only trying half-heartedly to attack him. They knew Oslan's prowess in the ring, and did not want to insult the throne by winning with what would be considered a cheap shot since the prince wasn't really fighting. There was no honor, nor glory in that. It was one thing to fight the prince of a kingdom when he could trounce most men with one hand tied behind his back. However, it was another matter altogether to kick a dog when it was down. Unfortunately for the king, Eurilas was well aware that not all of the knights fighting at the moment were from his kingdom. Many outsiders would not stop to think that they might be about to kill the only heir to the throne. The prince was expected to be able to fight. If he chose not to, well that was no fault of the knight that struck him down.

Oslan's horse sidestepped, narrowly missing a blow and saving them both from a potentially painful wound. Archer's wings flapped momentarily as he tried to keep his balance on Oslan's arm. Aylan called out in fear, and Oslan saw her. His whole body seemed to sigh a tired sigh, and he started moving his horse slowly toward her while fighting marginally better. He threw Archer into the air, and he started to climb high above his master. Oslan watched his progress, although his gaze seemed to continually return to Aylan as he fought knights to the left and right that were blocking his way toward her.

Then, a distraction: Aylan felt someone's eyes on her and she turned to see a smallish blond boy wearing the training insignia waiting to talk to her. "I beg your pardon?" Aylan asked, having missed the boy's first words.

"I said that I'm afraid I owe you an apology, Milady," the boy intoned. I misused your honor the other night, and I beg your forgiveness," the boy finished with a bow.

"Are you by chance named Aloysius?" Aylan coaxed.

The boy flushed to the roots of his yellow hair, clearly embarrassed that he had obviously been reported on. "Yes, Milady, I am he."

"Then go in peace Aloysius, but hold your tongue against me. For although I look different from most ladies you may be acquainted with, I *am* here now, and I assure you that I am quite capable of defending myself."

With a gulp, a nod and another bow, Aloysius left to await his turn in the arena with the rest of the knights in training.

It was then that Oslan reached her. He pulled his horse up beside the wall where she stood. "I have something of yours, I think." Oslan told her quietly. He pulled off his gauntlet and used his bare hand to reach under the breastplate of his armour. He withdrew her turquoise cloth. "Sasha came to me with this, saying that you wanted me to have it as a favour. I thought it odd that a favour from you would be brought by her. I would not let her attach it to me."

Does it surprise you that he would not accept a favour that was meant to have been from you? "Was this favour not good enough for you?" Aylan asked, tears making her vision blurry, as she took up the turquoise square of material. It was warm from being inside his armour, and gave off a faint scent of him.

"It would have made a fine token, I just could not accept it. I'm sorry if it really was your intent for her to give it to me." He replied.

At least I know now. He would not take what he thought was my favour. Though I wonder, was it because he wishes to remain unattached in the eyes of the king, the queen, or the whole kingdom? Or was it simply because it was from me? "I would have thought that your father would be proud, and any man would be filled with envy to see someone as beautiful as Sasha give you a favour." Aylan pointed out.

He sighed tiredly. "They would have been, but that was not Sasha's favour to give me. It was yours." He explained unhappily.

So there it is. Sasha is worthy, I am not. Had she had her own piece of cloth and not shown up with mine, I would have seen it tied to his armour and I could have saved him from having to explain. With her heart breaking, now the tears brimmed over Aylan's eyes. She had dared to let herself hope, and now she felt betrayed and anger at the prince's rejection rising.

She held the turquoise cloth between them in her fist, as if she were afraid that it might fly out of her grasp. "My father gave me this before he died. He was a great man much like the man I thought you were becoming," she shot at him. "He was fair, worked hard, and was a great knight. After he was gone, when I was a child, Mother used to plait it into my hair. My token is naught but an old swath of cloth, but it has been a symbol of love in my family, and is more than worthy of being a favour." she declared. *Why stop there?* She thought before she added: "I too might only be common, and I know that I might not be as glamorous as Sasha, but I am worthy too!"

The prince looked stricken. *She does not understand,* he thought, *does she actually think that I...I want...Sasha? How can she be so blind?* He reached out then, enfolding the hand holding the token in his own. The pain in her wrist flared again at the extra weight of his hand. She did not care. Her broken heart soared like his falcon above the arena as he continued, "Aylan, would you please give me a token of your favour?" he asked.

She blinked. *What games are these?* "It wasn't good enough for you five minutes ago, but now it is? I don't want you to ask for a token of my affection because I am upset. I think you miss the point."

"Aylan, it is you who has missed the point," he told her earnestly. "I do want a token of your affection, from you, only you. I would not want the kingdom to see Sasha tie a favour to my armour, for it is not from her that I seek the token of affection. I want the world to see that it is you who has seen fit to favour me over anyone else, that perhaps I am lucky enough to reside in your heart."

Aylan stared at the prince, dumbfounded. By degrees, what he said was starting to sink in. *He picked me?* she thought, *He wants me?* "What will your father say?" she asked, afraid. "The laws forbid us from being together. I am not a noble."

"Let me worry about Father. He loves me. He will want me to be happy. Kings can make laws, but they can also break them," he told her earnestly. "I have to go, there is a battle to be won, and I will win it not only for the kingdom, but for you."

Aylan tied her childhood treasure to her adult one. Wrapping the turquoise cloth twice around his arm and securing it in a double knot at his bicep, she wished him luck, as the ends fluttered in the breeze. Then she added: "One thing: should you find the occasion to kiss me again Oslan, my heart begs you to mean it. I do not like feeling like my lips are at your whim."

He told her as he made ready to trot back into battle: "I have meant every one. One day you will know that." He turned back to the battle, winking at her before he lowered his helmet's visor, replaced his gauntlet and charged back into the fray.

Her turquoise favour flapped in the wind as he rode away from her. He rode deftly in and around others' fights, until he found a space big enough to turn around. Over the clash of swords, maces, flails and spears, their eyes met. He laid his hand over his heart and extended it to her palm up. She remembered what he had told her about that sign: *"Lords and Ladies do this to tell their partners that they love them with their whole heart and that their heart belongs only to them."* She returned the gesture, missing the fact that the king was watching this exchange. She also missed the way he shook his head in disapproval.

Chapter 26
~ Archer to Archer, Dust to Dust ~

Oslan fought gallantly. As everyone present looked on, knights continued to fall, and clearly Oslan was back. His sword swung and blocked as a knight from another kingdom charged him. He steered his horse to sidestep, missing the blow. The other knight turned to face him again, calling him out as he panted from his run. "It's easy to fight a man from horseback, your Majesty. Why not bring yourself down to the lowly level of your commoners?"

Oslan was about to reply to the man with his sword, when Carn called to him "Behind you!"

Oslan had not seen the other man coming, but Carn had. While the knight on foot taunted the prince as a distraction, a second fighter, a huge ox of a man, had charged up behind him brandishing a great axe. Too late, Oslan turned just in time to see the second fighter about to bull rush him off of his steed. He received the impact badly and was thrown from his horse.

"Your Highness!" Carn called out at the sight of his leader and friend being flanked by two foes. "Don't let them surround-" but Carn's advice was cut off by a blow from a cavalier wearing a red cape, whose short sword had just pierced the side of the knight's armour. He went down. Instantly, Thornton and Bowregard ran out from a space in the stands to retrieve the downed Carn.

On the other side of the arena, the two brutes were only separated by a distance of twenty feet, with the prince dead centre in the middle of it. With a tiny rivulet of blood trickling down the left side of his face from the previous hit, Oslan stood to face them. He swung his sword around to test it, making ready for the fight on foot. His mind raced with battle stances, parries and strikes. He took a stance and urged them to come at him. The smaller of the two charged once again, leaving footprints in the sandy ground behind him. To Aylan who watched from her place by the wall, the attack came swiftly, but to the prince, everything seemed to move in slow motion. After four steps, the fellow was upon Oslan, who swung out with his sword. The man managed to dodge the sword-tip the first time, but was unable to hit the prince as he spun and moved. Oslan rounded on him, sword flashing in the sun. This time Oslan's weapon found its mark. It slammed into the side of the man's helmet, not penetrating, but knocking him out cold. The man went down, hard.

A "Boo!" went up in the crowd on the other end of the arena, and was accompanied by cries of "Leave 'em alone!" from the stands. Oslan turned toward the sound, where he saw the two archers trying to protect the downed Carn. Neither young man had weapons, as they were only there to help take the knights to the castle's herbologist for poultices to aid their healing. However, the fighter that had laid Carn down was not satisfied by his victory. He still brandished his sword, and stood at the ready, the corners of his red cape flapping listlessly in the small breeze. "I said move boys, or you will join your friend here on the ground," he bellowed. "The fight is not yet through if he still breathes."

"But Sir," young Thornton spoke up, bravely putting himself between Carn and the man with which he spoke, "He is a valiant knight, one of our kingdom's best, and this tournament is not a fight to the death. Once a man goes down, it is over. So say the rules."

The knight with the red cape scoffed at the boy, insulting the downed Carn as he lay moaning on the ground. "If this is the best your kingdom has to offer then I will be doing you a favour by putting him to rest. Ha, ha! Best? He couldn't best me! I'll show you what best looks like!" At that, he stepped toward Thorn in a menacing way, short sword ready to strike. Oslan saw it all. He left his own battle and took off toward the scene, but his speed on foot was no match for the short distance closing between Thorn and the sword.

Oslan let out a frantic high-pitched whistle as he ran, finding a way to pour on yet more speed. Clanging loudly in his heavy armour, he was beginning to grow weary but continued on nonetheless. Then, as the red caped man's sword flew toward Thorn, something heavy and solid fell out of the sky. The falcon slammed into the man's face, clawing and nipping. Seemingly all beak, claws and feathers, Archer beat the man about the head with his powerful wings. Off balance from the striking bird, the man toppled, landing in a wriggling pile beside Carn, who found occasion to smile through the pain at the sight. "Meet Archer," he informed the bully, "Apparently, *he* is the best one of us all! We will let him eat *your* portion of the feast at the banquet."

Oslan arrived to the man writhing under the bird, yelling: "Get it off, get it off, I withdraw!" Oslan whistled again and held up his gloved hand, calling the raptor to his arm. Archer immediately left off the man and returned to his master, whereupon he received a tasty treat from a leather pouch at the prince's side.

Beaming, Thornton thanked Oslan, and was finally able to work with Bowregard to get Carn to the hospice tent. They retreated, and Oslan watched as the clawed fighter was also escorted from the arena.

From the place he had just left, Oslan heard a feral scream: "Yeeeeraaah!" His previously huge opponent, if not large enough before, seemed to grow in size with new muscles and a renewed strength. "Don't walk away from me! I'm not done with you yet, cur!" he seethed at Oslan as spittle flew from his mouth. The battle around them had all but stopped, quieting the arena dramatically. By this point, the other fighting was done, these were the last two standing.

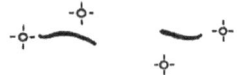

Chapter 27
~ Spitting Image ~

Oslan and the giant man faced off against each other, sweating inside their armour as the sun beat down upon them. The breeze had almost disappeared completely, making the day's heat hang in the air. Once again, Oslan launched Archer into the sky. The prince wasn't planning on calling on him again, but with the way these brutes were fighting, insurance was always a good thing to have. The ox of a man pointed his axe at the token on Oslan's arm. "I hope she's watching!" he growled.

"She will watch me decimate you," was Oslan's cool reply.

"Come on then!" challenged his opponent as he hefted his great axe.

Oslan ran at him then, with a surprising speed given all the weight of his armour he was carrying. Everyone saw the men come together. Aylan was surprised to see how Oslan had grown over the last few months. He had had new armour made, and indeed, he was now the size of a full grown man. However, he was not quite the size of this opponent that clearly dwarfed him. This hulk was losing control, and fear shot through Aylan as she watched, helpless to stop the fight before her.

As Oslan closed in and swung, the brute blocked his sword easily with the shaft of his great axe. Locked in battle, pushing against each other's weapon, Oslan could smell the stink of the other man as each fought to gain the upper hand. The man nodded toward the turquoise favour and spoke to Oslan in a low voice: "I am called Scringgen. I am a tracker, and I vow to you that once I finish with you, I will go find your lady. I will track her down and find her no matter where she hides."

Thinking of Aylan's magic and her invisibility pills, Oslan thought to himself *Yeah, good luck with that.* Outwardly though in order to keep her secret, he said: "She will be my queen one day, and every one of my knights will fight on her behalf. You would never reach her."

Misunderstanding, a gleam came to Scringgen's eye. "Ah, a princess!" he assumed. "Well that would make her twice as valuable to me. I will try twice as hard to lay you down like the whelp that you are!" he threatened, "Why don't you point her out to me now to save me the hassle of finding her later?" His eye travelled automatically to the dais that held the royal thrones. He searched the faces of the females that looked on. "Let me guess, it's the one in the pink dress, isn't it?"

Oslan felt the first stirrings of fear as he spied his sister Tanyan, looking lovely in pink despite the heat. Her lacy fan flicked quickly back and forth to cool her while she smiled encouragingly to him over it. Oslan's stomach churned. Tanyan was by far his closest sister, and he loved her dearly. Much unlike Aylan though, he knew her to be completely defenseless. For a split second, worry crossed his face and Scringgen took his chance.

With a forceful shove, Oslan was pushed back, needing to take a few steps in order to keep his balance. He recovered quickly though, and this time waited for Scringgen to come to him. The huge man circled, putting more space between them. Then with a roar, he attacked. The large man bore down on Oslan, axe held aloft ready to strike. Oslan held his pose, his own long sword neatly poised to counter the attack. He waited patiently, remembering his training. As Scringgen closed the gap between them, Oslan watched the great axe to see which way it would fall. Closer and closer still, came the massive man with the heavy weapon held above his head. Then came what Oslan was waiting for: the chop. A split second before the axe fell Scringgen pulled it back a few inches further to get more force behind it. The tip of the axe dipped to the right, and Oslan followed its move. Side-stepping and circling to the right, Oslan managed to dodge the heavy blow as the axe whistled down and to the left. He spun his long sword and slashed at the back of Scringgen's armour, causing him to fall forward on his face. Oslan kept his eye on the man as he struggled to rise off the ground under the weight of his plate armour.

Scringgen took the opportunity to both catch his breath and take another shot at the girl he believed to be the prince's Lady. "I yield, young prince," he said, holding up his hand to offer it to Oslan. The prince cautiously stepped forward, ready for a trick. As he reached for the man's arm to help him up, Scringgen's other hand flew up from the ground with a handful of dirt. The particles flew toward Oslan's visor as it had in practice. Scringgen pointed at Tanyan and called: "But I will still take your strumpet!" This time, everyone heard the comment that was flung across the distance like so much dirt. A collective gasp surrounded the arena.

Aylan's first instinct was to cast on the man, but found her arm would not rise. It was as if a band of unmovable steel was wrapped around her body and arms. She looked up at Lazelan, shock in her eyes. He shook his head almost imperceptivity at her as if to say *this is not your fight, you must not interfere.* Defeated, she relaxed and almost instantly the pressure on her arms dissipated.

Inside the arena, the dirt flung from Scringgen's hand hit Oslan's visor. Instead of Oslan falling back as Scringgen expected however, Oslan stepped forward. He placed his foot on Scringgen's right hand as it grasped the shaft of the great axe. The man's knuckles ground under Oslan's foot, but the prince did not let up. Instead, he bent low and whispered: "You really should stop insulting my sister, she is the daughter of the king and queen, and might have you imprisoned for your remarks." He dusted the dirt from his helmet's visor and continued: "By the way, I have seen that trick before. It is one of the reasons we wear visors. Here is the other." With this, Oslan brought the knee of his free leg up, connecting with Scringgen's nose. There was an audible crunch from the impact, and Scringgen howled in pain. Oslan let the man's hands free then to cup his broken nose. "Take him away!" he ordered and two guards came forth to take him first to the herbologist, then to the dungeon.

"Wait!" a feminine voice intoned from behind Oslan. He turned, raised his visor and was surprised to see his sister crossing the battlefield in her pretty pink dress, lacy fan still fluttering. She reached the spot where the guards stood on each side of Scringgen, who seemed to have diminished in size, and was looking all the worse for wear. The princess closed her fan and pulled on the handle, withdrawing from it a long dagger. With a short ringing *shink*, the dagger's blade emerged, whereby she held it fiercely to the man's throat. "I am Princess Tanyan, and I can assure you, *Sir*, that I am no strumpet! Know this now, that the next time you insult either me or my sisters, you will lose much more than your freedom!" She nodded at the guards and restated: "Now you may take him away!"

With the image of his sister, spitting mad and holding a dagger to a man's throat burned into his mind, Oslan stared, mouth agape. "Oh, close your mouth Oslan, you look like the fish that was served at last night's supper. Carn has been giving me lessons." She sighed, "I suppose Father will know now. He is going to have a fit."

"How did you manage to fit a dagger inside that bauble?" Oslan asked her privately.

"I had it made especially for just such an emergency. One can never be too cautious about one's honor. Speaking of which, you did wonderfully today. Father is almost bursting with pride." She let her finger trace over the silky material on her brother's arm. Pulling the cloth through her fingers and letting it fall, she added: "Well done indeed. I dare say that Father might put you in the stocks, but I'm sure she'll wait for you." Then she turned serious. "Whatever father thinks, know that I, that is, we girls, support you. I hope that I too will one day be able to find love."

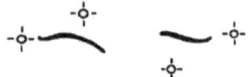

Chapter 28
~ Family Matters ~

After the day's melee combat, Oslan was requested to attend the king in the throne room. It was more an order than a request, really. Oslan approached the large double doors at a quick pace, undaunted. He had been summoned to the throne room before. Every time his father wished to scold him, actually. Eurilas felt that hard feelings should be kept out of their private chambers, so one always had a friendly place to retreat to in order to think things over after a lengthy discussion.

However, his father had also often called upon him there in order to congratulate him on a task well done. Oslan felt rather confident, having won the day's tournament event, but was still curious as to what this was going to be about. Outside, he squared his shoulders and took a deep breath to steady himself. He took the last three steps to the door and was forced to dodge quickly to the side as it swung outward, narrowly missing him.

Lazelan appeared, looking tired and diminished.

"He is in no good mood, I am afraid," he told Oslan as they passed in the hall.

"What has happened?" he enquired of his old friend, letting the heavy throne room doors swing shut again without entering.

"I have given your father some rough news I'm afraid. He is not taking it well. I regret to tell you, Your Highness-"

"Oslan, please!" Oslan corrected.

"I regret to tell you, Oslan," Lazelan continued, "that my time with you has come to an end. Sasha has had a vision. She knows who it is that threatens your kingdom and my Magdolyn. I must return to her post haste. Your father is having his men prepare a ship to take me home. I leave in a fortnight. We must meet tonight to seek ways to protect your home until the situation has been made right."

Oslan took the news like a blow. "I will meet you when I am through with my father," he promised.

Lazelan nodded in thanks. "I spoke with him in private, but I am sure he is ready for you now." Then he added a low "Good luck," patting his friend on the shoulder before he continued down the hall, heading Oslan supposed, to his laboratory to start packing up his things.

Oslan took a deep breath and opened the door before him. As the door swung outward and he passed through the doorway, he beheld the impressive king dressed in red with black flecked white fur trim, sitting on his throne at the far end of the room. Oslan walked under the vaulted ceiling, treading confidently as the red carpet runner dampened the sound of his foot falls on the way to the throne. He moved passed huge round pillars that reached from ceiling to floor, past the lavish tapestries that hung grandly on the walls, and past guards and throngs of gaudily dressed courtiers. Lords and ladies adorned this room as often as allowed, trying to curry favour with the king while they gossiped and waited to hear the goings on of the royal family. Guards too were always present to protect the king since the days before Gorin's attack on the patriarch.

The prince finished his journey through the long room and stood before the king at the base of the stairs leading up to the thrones' dais. "You asked to see me, Sire?" he enquired, always using the more formal title around the public.

"Yes Oslan," the king began, "We need to talk about that little display at the tournament."

"Oh, I don't know, Sire, I think I did alright for myself!" Oslan boasted, avoiding the real topic that was lurking under the unsaid words. "I did leave as the last man standing!"

"Indeed," replied Eurilas, with a nod of approval and a hint of pride in his voice. Then he cleared his throat and continued, "However, that is not the display I was referring to." The king shook his head as he gestured to the turquoise cloth that still hung from Oslan's arm like a banner.

"I thought you would be happy, Sire. You have been so adamant that I marry lately. Are you not overjoyed to learn that I have finally felt affection for a lady?"

The king sighed tiredly, placing both palms face down on the golden arms of his throne. "Therein lies the problem, Oslan. She dresses like a man and has no station. She is not a noble lady."

"But Sire, I can assure you that she is quite noble!" Oslan protested in jest, pushing his father's temper just a little. "Why just the other day she-"

"Enough!" the king roared, getting the attention of any courtier that to this point had not been listening. "You will not defy me, son!"

"Love matters! Family matters!" Oslan tried to make him see. "Surely you understand that love will make a family and therefore a kingdom stronger. You can't expect me to marry simply for station. I have found *love*!"

"Not another word!" the king said evenly as he looked Oslan levelly in the eye. Then he stood as he made his decree, "You will choose a wife that I approve of by the end of the feast, or I will appoint one for you!"

Oslan turned white as a sheet. "But Father,"

he gaped openly as his hands fell to his sides. "You can't do this!"

The courtiers in the room gasped at the open defiance to the throne.

"I may be your father, but I am also King!" Eurilas' voice boomed. "When you take the crown, you may make all the rules you want, marry an impure strumpet for all I care, but until then I am your ruler!"

"How would that help me?" Oslan questioned, his voice cracking. "I must marry *before* I take the throne! If I am already married when I become king, how am I supposed to make it so that I can marry whom I wish? It is not possible!" came Oslan's outburst.

"Then I suppose, Son, that this topic of discussion is closed," Eurilas replied sternly.

Oslan's face burned red. His hands clenched into fists of rage at his sides, he turned stiffly and retreated quickly down the carpet runner toward the door. Aylan's telltale turquoise cloth now seemed to mournfully wave goodbye to Eurilas from the air current of Oslan's hurrying away. *I am truly sorry, son. Following decorum is an evil necessity of being royalty,* the king thought sadly as Oslan slipped out of the throne room before his hot tears could betray him.

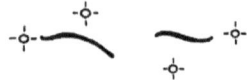

Chapter 29
~ Mirror, Mirror on the Wall,
Who Will Make Our Kingdom Fall? ~

Oslan quickly made his way to Lazelan's laboratory to see why his friend was so suddenly running home. The way he felt right now, he wished he could take Aylan away and join him. The prince had already returned to his chambers to wash the dust and sweat off of himself from the tournament. The hot water that the servants brought had helped to sooth his muscles and calm his emotions. Now, instead of seething anger, he only felt a quiet sadness, and a firm resolve. Before he had removed his armour, he had carefully untied and kept Aylan's turquoise token. Later, he had sat on his bed regarding it while he held it in his hands. *It is amazing how such a small thing can represent so much,* he thought. *Love, hope, and after talking to Father, perhaps the destruction of the happy future I've always wanted.*

In his inner chamber Oslan had a writing desk, and in the middle drawer there was a panel that opened. The drawer had a false bottom, so that anyone that looked in would see a drawer full of the prince's usual belongings – parchment, quills, an ink pot, sealing wax etc. But under all of this, the panel hid the real bottom of the drawer, which left a small space where things could be hidden. This is where he placed his most sacred treasures: the first gold coin his father had ever given him, a lock of hair from his first haircut, a likeness of his mother and sisters, one of his falcon's downy baby feathers. He had gone to his secret hiding spot, opened it, and then he had added Aylan's carefully folded turquoise length of cloth to his mix of treasures. There it currently rested, safe and sound.

Now, Oslan reached for the laboratory's door. Pulling it open, he came across his friends, Lazelan, Sasha and of course, Aylan. Instead of finding them packing as he had expected though, they were huddled around the worktable, regarding a wide, low bowl of water. They all looked up upon his noisy entrance.

"Oslan, you broke my spell!" Aylan admonished, though showed no outward signs of hostility. In fact, Sasha noted the slight blush that had risen on Aylan's cheeks as the prince entered.

"Ah, but you are doing much better," Lazelan encouraged while gently giving her arm a squeeze. "You know you are ready to do this job," he added as he turned to the far wall. He walked over and motioned for her to join him. "And, I think you're ready for this." He turned to the other two in the room. "Friends, would you please turn your backs to us? There are some tricks that must be kept between mages."

Sasha and Oslan gave each other a puzzled look turning their backs to the two mages and heard Lazelan speak in the old magical tongue: "Uti tax tari halix rik, shoatmai lan tayt ertae sulta." He paused then, and added in a commanding voice "Relik!" Then, there was silence. After a few moments of hearing nothing, the sound of shuffling feet followed and then Lazelan spoke once more: "Sot!"

Then it was Aylan's turn to speak. "Please rejoin us at the table." Sasha and the prince turned to find Aylan leaning a gigantic mirror up against a bare wall between two candleholders. Sasha started. 'Where did that come from?"

Aylan set the mirror down gently so it leaned against the wall and reflected all of their faces. Then she turned and waved her hands mysteriously in the air and said jokingly: "Magic!"

In reality, Lazelan had taken Aylan over to a bare wall that was devoid of shelves. He had spoken to her in Almatrae and now fluent, Aylan had understood it: *This is a secret room, meant for your eyes only.* He had lightly tapped the wall in the centre three times with two fingers and commanded: *"Open!"* Then a section of the wall had swung into a void like a door. Beyond it was another room, darkened and musty. He had entered, turned to a four-foot mirror and picked it up, hefting it over to her. It had beautiful gilt edges woven in an intricate vine pattern. He had handed it to her, tapped the door of the passage three times again and commanded, *"Close!"* The wall had silently swung shut and sealed completely; leaving no trace that there was ever a break in the wall.

Once the mirror was positioned, Aylan regarded herself in it. She had grown so much over the last year, and without her mother around to constantly nag her about how shaggy her hair was getting, it had grown now quite long past her shoulder blades. She made a mental note to start tying it back so it would look neater.

"Oslan, there has been a discovery. Aylan, show him Ethik as you showed us." Lazelan instructed. Aylan nodded her response.

Standing in front of the mirror, Aylan outstretched her hand and waved it across the surface of the mirror, saying "Vearta uta da Ey seche ot isa. Vearta Ethik." *Reveal that which I seek to see. Reveal Ethik.* Then, with a glance at Lazelan, she added: "Vearta Zaltreous." *Reveal Zaltreous.* The reflection of the four swirled and twisted on the mirror's surface before solidifying into a new image. Sasha was ready for it, but Oslan gasped when the mirror changed. Aylan held her focus on what she was doing though, and concentrated hard enough that she didn't lose her spell.

The scene in the mirror now showed a man Lazelan's age with sleek black hair and a beige shirt made out of a light summery material. He sat hunched over his desk, pouring over the writings in the thick book that sat there. The words were clear in the image, but were not in the common language of the land.

"Who is he?" Oslan asked, gesturing to the man.

"Currently, he is the biggest threat to your kingdom that we know of," Lazelan reported gravely.

"What threat?" Oslan inquired, alarmed, "He must be leagues away in a distant land, your land I'd wager."

"How do you know that?" Aylan asked, shocked, as Oslan didn't speak Almatrae to her knowledge, and the only thing the image revealed was Zaltreous at his desk. She reasoned that to anyone that didn't know where the spell focused, he would seem to be in any old stone room, right next door, perhaps.

"Look at the window beside him." Oslan pointed out. "Those plants growing outside are ones that I have never seen in my kingdom, nor have I seen them in the surrounding kingdoms when I've visited them on trips. Then there is the matter of his clothes. He is dressed much the way you were when you were shipwrecked and brought to my home, Lazelan."

His three companions started at his observation. They were so focused only on Lazelan what he was doing, that they had missed what could have been important information in the bigger picture. "It is mine," Lazelan shared, "I lent him that shirt. It was very much in fashion in Ethik when I left." They looked closer at the image and sure enough, there was half of a window in the wall to the side of their subject, cut off where the image stopped. Large green leaves of some type of fern waved and bobbed in an invisible wind outside the window.

Lazelan leaned over to Aylan and said in a low voice: "Let this be a lesson to all of us, we shouldn't lose sight of the whole picture. There may be important details to be missed that could help us keep this kingdom safe." Then to Oslan in a louder voice, he continued: "Sasha has seen that this man is plotting against the kingdom. She came to me right away to see if I could confirm this for her. It was him that attacked the peasants during the sky-fire display."

"This is the powerful mage you spoke of? Why does he threaten us?" Oslan demanded.

Lazelan looked weary. He sat with his elbows on the worktable. He let his face fall into his upturned hands, so that his short red hair just curled around the tips of his fingers. "Sasha has learned that he is after Magdolyn," he confessed, "Maggie stands by me though, and because of this, his plan has changed. He will try to dethrone your father and take the kingdom for himself. Someone put the idea into his head that if he were king, he could marry anyone he chooses."

At this, Oslan scoffed, "That seems to be the common idea right now." He announced, thinking of his own father's view. "But why does he attack us, why not a kingdom closer? For that matter, why not just take over his own kingdom? Why does he want mine?" he questioned.

"I am afraid that we sealed our doom when we thwarted his flaming packet attack," Lazelan confided, "He sought not only to take Magdolyn from me, but my job too. He was trying to prove me incompetent in front of your father. That didn't work. It is not enough for him to win in anything, he must crush the competition. That is Zaltreous' way, it always has been."

Aylan had been studying the image in the mirror the whole time she listened, and now she spoke: "Lazelan, look!" Aylan began, "I can read some of what he studies. Does that really say postokia?" Aylan thought, *this is dark and powerful magic indeed.* Out loud, she continued: "Can he use that on people he scries, like he affected the packets on the night of the sky explosion display?"

"Perhaps," Lazlelan answered, his voice low, "we will have to guard against it."

Sasha piped up then, concerned, "What does postokia mean?" she asked while looking slowly from one mage to the other.

Lazelan and Aylan gazed at each other, weighing the weight of their words. Then, they turned to their friends. "It is a possession spell," they answered in unison.

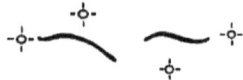

Chapter 30
~ Sent Packing ~

"What does a possession spell do exactly?" Sasha asked, afraid.

"This possession spell would allow him to take over someone else's body," Aylan explained, "If he scried you Oslan, then he could cast the possession spell on you. Then, everything he would want you to say and do, you would do. It would be like you had lost control of your body, and you would be powerless to stop him, you would just kind of be there, watching it all unfold."

"He could make me challenge my father for the crown," Oslan stated in horror. "Then I would have to fight him to the death. What if I killed him?"

"Zaltreous could do that, but that wouldn't help him." Aylan reassured him. "Either one of you could win a fight for the crown. It would be too risky. It would be much simpler for him to use the spell to take over Eurilas himself, and make him relinquish his crown outright. He could even make the king name Zaltreous as the successor in open court."

The group of four friends sat stunned, taking in the implications of such a spell. "He won't be able to possess the king if we can find another way to protect him from such things," Lazelan replied, doubtfully. "The only problem is that he is reading a book of great evil. It is called the *Almatraek Dim*, as it was fashioned from dark magic. It contains very powerful spells, some of which can only be countered by spells from its sister book, the *Almatraek Bright*, which we don't have. Mages of good began to compile a list of antidotes, charms, and spells to repair, prevent, and counteract the evil done from spells found within the *Almatraek Dim*.

There would be a ward in it to protect the king from being possessed by a spell from the *Almatraek Dim*. From what I understand though, the *Almatraek Bright* has been lost for years. Its guardian put it into hiding to prevent it from falling into the hands of the keeper of the other book. It waits somewhere, to be found by someone who will protect it and use it for good."

"I know of the *Almatraek Dim*," Oslan admitted, surprising them all. "Carn followed its progress while it was being made, and intercepted a few scrolls before they could be added to the book. Carn returned to us, his quest for the book ended when he got reports that the ship that had been carrying it had gone down. There was no trace of the book after that, so he assumed that the book had been lost to the sea. It appears now that that was not the case."

"What if you were to put a spell on the king so that no one could scry him?" Sasha suggested.

Lazelan shook his head, "That would save the king from being possessed, but it wouldn't stop Zaltreous from possessing the queen, or one of the prince's sisters, or even Oslan. The king could be forced to hand over the crown under duress if the queen suddenly climbed into a window and threatened to jump if he didn't. We simply don't have the power to cast spells on everyone that might influence your father. Even if Aylan and I worked together to do so, it might kill us and the magic would disappear if we were to die anyway." Lazelan reasoned.

"We can't shield everyone from being possessed because the anti-possession spells are in the *Almatraek Bright,* which we don't have." Aylan thought aloud as she ticked problems off on her fingers. "We are not powerful enough to cast the amount of spells necessary to shield everyone anyway. We don't know who he will strike at, so we can't protect just the king." She pondered these things, and then she had a moment of clarity. "Zaltreous can't possess them if he can't see them. So why don't we use simple herbology to make everyone invisible? Then he won't be able to scry them in the first place." Aylan struck the top of the table with the side of her fist in triumph.

"Can you imagine the havoc that would wreak on my kingdom?" Oslan protested. "Servants would bang into each other just walking across the room! Besides, people would forget to take a pill and become visible, and some folk don't trust magic and would flatly refuse, how would that help?"

But during the prince's speech, Lazelan began to nod slowly, looking at Aylan. "She doesn't mean make the people invisible to each other, only to him." Lazelan countered.

"But how? Sasha asked, "Is it possible?"

"By solving all of our problems at once," Aylan remarked, "We make a mixture of herbs that will block only scrying, not possession. We can pack the mixture into pouches. If we hide them in every room of the keep, the rooms become invisible and everyone in each room falls under its protection. The non-believers will never be the wiser, yet Zaltreous could not scry anyone here to cast upon. In essence, he will no longer be able to find the castle."

"Like a blank spot on a map!" Sasha added excitedly.

Oslan rounded the table and took Aylan in his arms, hugging her. She melted inside as she stood awkwardly, his embrace holding her arms to her sides. "Thank you," he breathed into her hair, "Thank you for saving my kingdom."

"Don't mention it!" she managed in a whisper, "at least not until the packets are in place. We will need some herbs from the forest, and we will need help packing the pouches."

The prince released her and looked at his three friends. "Carn and I will see that it is done," the prince assured them. He left them then to collect the supplies he would need to complete packing the pouches. All of them saw his one backward glance toward Aylan as he quitted the laboratory.

Once he was gone, Sasha confronted Aylan, wanting to know everything. "You two have reconciled?" she demanded, raising an eyebrow, "Tell me how, I have to know! The whole balance of this kingdom's future happiness depends on your reconciliation!" she said dramatically.

"Yes," was all that Aylan gave her.

Internally, Sasha was going crazy. Outwardly poised, as always, she returned a stray lock of blond hair to its rightful place behind her ear, and hinted at her failure with the turquoise favour, "I did what I could, but he resisted. I thought the two of you were lost to each other. Now you have reunited, what did you do that I could not?"

Aylan tried to seem cross that Sasha had stolen her precious cloth, though the thought of Oslan riding around on that field while wearing her favour brought joy to her heart. "Don't you know what happened?" she teased, "Aren't you supposed to be able to find this stuff out for yourself?" she asked instead of answering.

Sasha gave up, accepting the fact that things would be alright, the future was once again secure for Endalwynndale. "How will you get around his father's disapproval? Oslan hasn't yet told you what his father has said, has he?" she hedged, changing the subject only slightly. When Aylan confirmed that Oslan had said nothing, Sasha relayed the conversation that had taken place in the throne room.

Aylan seemed to take it in stride. "I might be a common girl," Aylan started, "but I have the uncanny ability to do uncommon things. As for the approval of King Eurilas, we have a plan, but I will need both of you to help." Lazelan and Sasha agreed instantly as Aylan had suspected they would. "What must we do?" Lazelan queried.

"I need you to teach me one more spell," she told Lazelan, "and you," she added looking to Sasha, "will need to go borrow a dress fit for a princess."

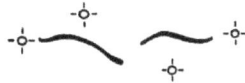

Chapter 31
~ Playing Ball ~

With the pouches distributed throughout the castle, and the shutters closed in Aylan's little room, the quartet felt secure that no one was watching. The prince sat on the floor of Aylan's chambers, his back leaning up against her bed. Birdsong and sunlight streamed in through the slats in the closed shutters. The dust motes danced in and out of the slatted sun, which created blades of light cutting through the dark. The room was lit with a bright blue glow as Oslan tried to make it seem as if he was manipulating a glowing orb that floated in the air in front of him. The orb was big enough that he could just hold it in one hand, but the hard part for Oslan was that he could not feel the orb, he could only see it. Their trick was based on Oslan's ability to make it look like he was actually holding it. He was going to have to fool everyone in order to make their plan for the banquet work.

As Aylan concentrated on keeping the illusion spell going, Lazelan and Sasha encouraged Oslan and gave him pointers to help make what he was doing look more realistic. They were trying to make it look as though Oslan was holding the orb, and throwing it up and catching it. Aylan was trying to maintain the spell while moving the orb up and down in the air at the right time, as if the prince were controlling its movements.

"This would be so much easier if I could feel it. My eyes see it, but my hands feel nothing there." Oslan complained as his fingers once again seemed to curl into the ball.

"Aylan doesn't have the strength to add more tactile sensations to the orb and create the spell again at night." Lazelan countered, "Each new sensation; sound, taste, smell, and touch, that she adds to the illusion makes the spell all the more difficult to maintain, and will drain her energy that much more quickly. She will already have to draw from my strength tonight as it is to do what we have planned.

They practiced for another hour before they figured the prince and Aylan were ready. By the time they were done, Aylan could appear to throw the ball at him and he could seem to catch it. He could roll it down his arms and hold it. Most importantly, he could walk, skip and dance with it. "Ok, I think you've had enough." Lazelan finally said, releasing the prince to go prepare for the banquet that was to take place in a few hours. The prince took his leave, and the three that remained went on to practice phase two of their plan. Sasha excused herself to put on the dress she had secured from Oslan's oldest sister, Talithan.

"How do you feel?" Lazelan asked her when they were alone.

"Exhausted," Aylan answered truthfully.

"I have another secret of mage work to share with you Aylan," Lazelan remarked, "But it is very risky, and if not taken seriously, you could accidently harm a lot of people badly."

Aylan contemplated this as Lazelan elaborated: "It can be dangerous for those you cast it on, not for you. Your heart is pure, and I know you would never let those under your protection come to harm. This is why I choose to share this with you now. If a mage needs to draw upon more power than they have, there is a way to draw power from everyone and almost everything around you. Anything with a life-force can contribute to your spells, giving you energy and helping you to sustain it longer. Using this trick can also help you cast spells that are too powerful for you to cast alone."

"What do I ask them to do to make it work?" Aylan asked naïvely.

"You don't," Lazelan replied grimly, "You cast on them and just take it from them. This is what I'm afraid Zaltreous has been planning to do in order to cast his possession spell, but *he* won't stop until he succeeds."

"What happens to the people you borrow life-force from?" Aylan questioned, although she thought she already knew the answer.

"The same thing that would happen to you if you used too powerful a spell. It could kill them. When using this spell, it is imperative that you keep gauging the people you have used, if any of them seem weak, you must release them, whether your spell is complete or not. Only experienced mages use this trick because it is so difficult to concentrate on two spells at once, as well as keep an eye on those under its influence."

"Can mages borrow life force from trees and animals?" Aylan asked.

Lazelan nodded, "They can, and in fact, it is why some mages travel with a pet. They would always have that little bit of extra power to draw from. However, animals, unless large sized, do not have very much to give, and can't tell you when they are feeling weak. Many mages have inadvertently killed their pets in the past, so most mages don't rely on them anymore as a power source. Trees contain much power, however, they give off no outward signs that they are weakening. It would be easy to wipe out a whole forest without realizing you are doing it. Then you would be responsible also for the deaths of all the animals that rely on that forest to live."

Aylan thought about this for a long time. "I

can see why people are the best choices, but why would you not just ask first?" she questioned.

"People might change their minds, conjure side effects that don't actually exist, or might turn you in, claiming at some later time that you had injured them in some way. Using this spell will leave no lasting effect on those it is targeted on. However, ignorant people love to jump at shadows. Let's pretend you were still a farmer that had no knowledge of real magic. Someone asked to cast a spell on you. You agreed and everything went well. Then a few negative things happened to you in your life. Perhaps your crop failed, or your cow died. Perhaps your well went dry or you lost part of your herd of sheep. It would be easy for you as a farmer to make the leap that you had been cursed. In a day when most people do not know of the workings of true magic of the mind, it is easily misunderstood by those that fear it. If rumours that the mage is cursing people circulated in a kingdom, you would be punished or perhaps have to flee. Trust me, it is better for folk to be kept in the dark, for your own safety."

"How will I ever know if I am ready to use something like that?" Aylan thought aloud.

"I would like you to try it tonight at the ball," Lazelan coaxed.

"But Lazelan," she protested, "what if I hurt someone? I don't think I could live with that."

Lazelan smiled at his pupil then, knowing he had made the right choice in telling her. "I will be there to help. I will watch with you, if someone is not strong enough and you miss it, I will break your concentration so no one gets hurt."

The door opened then, and Sasha walked in. Now it was time for Aylan to practice again. Her task was to add the sensations of smell, touch and sound to the orb. She asked Sasha to move around so she could hear the rustle of the glamorous dress.

Chapter 32
~ A Change in Plans ~

Zaltreous had been trying all afternoon to scry the king to put his plan in motion. In fact, when that didn't work, he tried the queen, then the rest of the royal family. He became more and more outraged as the scope of his abilities seemed to have been blocked. He finally gave up after being unsuccessful with scrying the castle or grounds. He understood now that his plan had been found out. *They are far more resourceful than I gave them credit for.* He mused, *I must find another way. I will not be stopped.* He let his spell cast a wider net, trying to see the country, then only the outer villages, then the lands surrounding the castle. He found a blind spot, a bubble of land that could not be seen by the spell. He scanned the countryside and determined that the castle and its inhabitants had been the only things that escaped his sight. *I will show them that I too can be resourceful,* he thought. He could not scry the castle, so instead he scried the road leading up to it. After a while, people began arriving in fancy outfits of lavish materials and light colours. All afternoon this continued, and to Zaltreous it became obvious that there was going to be a ball.

This makes my job even easier! He elated. There would be many people entering the castle, but not many people should be leaving, as the servants would be hard at work preparing for the guests. He couldn't possess a guest going in, as he would lose sight of them once they entered, and there was no guarantee that they would have access to the king anyway. He required a servant that was familiar with the workings of the castle. After an hour of watching somewhat listlessly, he finally saw what he had been waiting for.   One of the palace kitchen servants popped into view as he exited the castle grounds. He was carrying a basket, and was moving quite quickly against the host of people arriving at the palace.

Zaltreous followed the man's progress until he reached the market. A wicked smile spread over Zaltreous' face as his plans changed once more. He wouldn't need a possession spell after all. *All I will need will be a little power of suggestion.* He thought as he remembered another incantation from the book of dark magic on his desk. This could be a much tamer spell than the one he had planned on using, but Zaltreous decided to pour it on strong, just in case the servant had any scruples. As the man shopped, Zaltreous cast a spell that would charm him into doing his bidding. He started out small with his commands, to see if the man would indeed follow his orders.

In the marketplace, the servant that had been buying last minute fresh ingredients for that night's feast, stopped with an apple half way to his basket. He stood still for a moment as if listening then shook his head as if to clear it. He paid for his fruit, and walked on to another stall. On the way, he suddenly seemed to have an idea: *I should buy some scorchroot.* He entered a nearby tent full of herbs, spices and charms. The crone behind the counter eyed him doubtfully. He was obviously wearing the castle livery, and she wanted no part in any transaction that would result in her being sent to the dungeon. It was odd for a castle servant to be in her tent anyway, since the king's kitchen used only herbs grown in the king's forest. "I would like to buy some of your finest scorchroot," he announced. Now here was a surprise.

"What was that? I'm sorry sir, but my hearing

isn't as grand as it used to be, I thought that I heard you ask for some scorchroot," she announced.

"Indeed I did. Come, come now woman, don't keep me waiting. I must get back to the castle post haste," the servant insisted.

"Now what would you be needing scorchroot for? It's very deadly, ye ken."

"Let's just say that we have a rat problem to deal with."

Shocked, she went behind her counter and pulled out a long thin root that resembled a small parsnip, though it had red veins coursing down the length of it. He paid for the root and turned back to the crone as he was about to leave the tent.

"One more thing, how much of this do I need to use in order to kill the rat?" he enquired as he hid the root under the apples in his basket.

"Not very much at all, Sir. In fact, if a few shavings are boiled down and even a single drop is fed to one, it will kill even a very *large* rat." She finished the last two words with a wink, and the man left. She decided to close shop for the day, just in case someone was watching.

Back outside in the sunlight, the servant blinked a few times against the sun. He traversed the market, weaving in and around people bustling by him.

One more test, thought Zaltreous from his room leagues away in a distant land. The servant in the market started heading back toward the castle. On the way by a stand selling jewelry, he promptly swiped a necklace off the table and kept walking, hiding it in his basket. In his room, Zaltreous' smile grew even wider. The servant made it back to the castle grounds without being searched or discovered. He then received one final command before crossing under the entrance's portcullis, where Zaltreous' mirror could show no more.

Chapter 33
~ Healthy Competition ~

That night's banquet was stupendous. The music was jovial and the musicians were pristine. The courtiers were dressed in the newest fashions, richest fabrics, light coloured clothes and bright jewels. The men looked swanky and the ladies looked lovely. Aylan was impressed at the transformation of the knights, who had been covered in dirt and blood in the arena the day before, but were now wearing their best and looking trim and proper for this special occasion. Aylan, as usual, wore a man's tunic, although even she had had this one made new for the event. She had even managed to smooth her hair back into a pony tail, which left her looking quite pretty in the end. Lazelan sat to Aylan's left once more, although Sasha, who never missed a party, was nowhere to be found. "She didn't want to steal your thunder," Lazelan informed her, looking dashing in a tunic that was only now being worn for the first time.

The king stood and declared the tournament over, presenting to the court the winners of each event. Bowregard had won the archery contest, and Oslan had won events in both the melee combat as well as an exhibition of falconry. Carn had taken the prize for the joust, and an outsider from another village had won the chariot race. Aylan did not see much of Millie, as she was spending a copious amount of time trying to console her brother Thornton, who had not done as well as he had hoped in the archery contest. In fact, he had still insisted on using his father's bow, and had only hit the target twice.

Then the food was served. Carried out from the kitchen by a succession of servers, there were many delights to choose from. The guests piled their bread trenchers high with fish, fowl and pork, stews and broths. Cheese was also offered, a rare delicacy in this kingdom. Aylan could see and taste that the king had spared no expense. The bakers brought a large pastry in the shape of a castle, and a variety of apples, pears and other fruits which were baked as a dessert.

When everyone had eaten their fill, the tables were cleared away, and men started to ask ladies to dance. To Oslan's dismay, throngs of girls of every shape and size presented themselves to him, giving him barely enough time to breathe. It was obvious that some noble women had spent a fortune on new dresses, shoes, and baubles for their daughters to wear. Each one tried to catch his attention with the extravagance of their hair, and outfits that screamed wealth. Mothers in the crowd sent over their daughters, shouting instructions at them: "Smile! Don't fidget! Say something interesting! Invite him for tea!"

Then Oslan made a bold move, conscious of the fact that it would enrage his father. He stood from his throne and with a soft "If you will excuse me please ladies," he walked through the group of them straight to where Aylan now stood on the sidelines of the dance floor. As the confused ladies stood before the dais, and the prince moved slowly away from them, Lazelan leaned over and said to Aylan: "It is almost time, are you ready?"

"As ready as I'll ever be," Aylan responded automatically. Oslan arrived then, and after a glance to make sure his family was watching, he smoothly took Aylan's hand and bent low over it, kissing the back. Aylan thought that he let his lips linger there a little longer than was typical, but with the way the touch of his soft kiss made her heart slam into her rib cage; she found she didn't mind in the least.

"It worked," came Lazelan's whisper, "He is talking with your mother, and pointing in your direction. He really seems incensed."

Oslan grinned, "I haven't had this kind of fun in years," the prince admitted. "He'll be fine momentarily, it's almost time for the magic to happen. Just before you do, though…" The prince let his voice trail off and before she could cast anything, he grabbed both of her hands and whisked her out onto the dance floor. "You can't blame me for wanting one dance with you before I lose you, can you?"

Aylan shook her head and allowed him to hold her close. *My hand seems to fit perfectly in his*, she thought, content. With one arm around her back, and the other held to the side, Oslan led her around on the dance floor to the beat of the music the troubadours played. Eventually, the music stopped and Oslan returned her to Lazelan's side.

"Now, before another song begins!" Lazelan instructed, "First cast the energy spell, then the other. Focus on as many people as you can, the more people you borrow energy from, the less you will have to use from any of them."

Aylan did as she was told. She tried to see the room as a whole. Keeping her hands down this time, she closed her eyes and said the incantation as Lazelan had taught it to her: "taritae tritae nula kraku, tigo Ey tayt tiris." *All points of power, lend me your strength*. Energy surged through her, and she was surprised to learn that her spell's focus was still strong though she sent the spell directly from her core instead of channeling it through her palm. She was becoming more skilled after all. Everything was becoming easier. Outwardly, she smiled to keep up appearances for Oslan. She opened up her eyes and looked around. The people in the ballroom continued to dance and mingle as if nothing had happened. *And now,* she thought, *the real work begins.*

She cast the second spell and watched the door. A beautiful girl materialized, seeming to step in through the doorway from outside. She was simply radiant. Dressed in a deep turquoise blue gown that contrasted with the lighter colours of the other girls' dresses, she clearly stood out from the rest of the eligible girls in the crowd. Her blond hair was curled and plaited in intricate patterns that looked as if it had taken days to complete. Her beautiful eyes shone blue, and stood out nicely against flawless soft skin that almost seemed to glow. Her dainty nose and high cheekbones gave her a regal look that was only accentuated by her full pouty lips. The swoop of her dress' bodice was styled precisely to draw the eye, but did so tastefully. The flowing gown swayed slightly as the young lady walked, and drew everyone's attention. People's conversations died down and returned in a babble as she surveyed the throng of girls, and found Oslan with her eyes.

Beside Aylan, Oslan was staring, open mouthed, jaw hanging down.

"Be careful my prince", Aylan told him, "I think if you drool any more, you might create a new moat," she finished smugly. Oslan let his mouth snap shut.

"You'd better go get her before another man asks her to dance." Lazelan advised. Oslan audibly gulped and stepped forward. "Wish me luck," he begged as he walked toward the beauty before him.

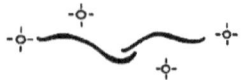

Chapter 34
~ Sealed With a Kiss ~

Oslan closed the gap between them rapidly. From their places on the throne, the king, queen, and Oslan's three sisters watched as he bowed deeply from the waist and offered the lady his hand. She nodded gracefully and accepted the proffered hand, blushing slightly.

"Nice touch," Lazelan complimented sideways as he saw the girl's colour change. Aylan only nodded, concentrating very hard on the couple on the dance floor. The prince gingerly laid his hand on the lady's back as he held the other out to the side. He watched her every movement, and played his part beautifully. Whenever they neared another dancing couple, Oslan would hear the swish of her skirts.

On the dais, the princesses waited for the other girls to go back to their mothers, which they all did after realizing that they were no competition for the beauty in blue. Talithan, Tanyan and Trindalynn finally made their own way out onto the dance floor with partners of their own. Through the music and mingling, and even when dancing, Tanyan kept a watchful eye on Aylan. Tanyan could see Aylan staring nonstop at the couple. She appeared to be concentrating on them desperately, and kind Tanyan's heart went out to Aylan. She liked the girl, woman now really, and had been secretly hoping her father would have allowed the marriage despite her upbringing. *I ought to go over and console the poor dear,* she thought, and excused herself from her dance partner to do so. She walked primly, head up as a princess should, and was so focused on Aylan that she didn't see the tray and serving girl coming at her from the side. With a mighty clatter, Millie tipped her tray, spilling its contents onto the unfortunate princess. Millie apologized profusely and guided Tanyan from the room to help her find her own ladies in waiting so she could change.

"That was a close one." Lazelan said as he breathed a sigh of relief. "It's a good thing Thorn is more proficient at singing and playing lute than he is archery. If he wasn't performing next, Millie might still have been consoling him, and would not have been around to keep interference away. If Tanyan had made it over here, she may have tried to rescue you from the sight of Oslan with another woman by asking you to walk with her in the gardens as she is prone to doing. It wouldn't do to have your illusion suddenly disappear in the middle of the dance floor as you left."

Eventually, after the dancing was almost done, the troubadours took a brief break to switch musicians. During that time, a servant approached Oslan, whispering in a low voice that the king wished for an introduction with the young Lady. Oslan led the image of perfection toward the dais to make the announcement of a lifetime. "I suppose it's about time that I meet the king," she mused quietly, "Since I have been living in his castle for over a year now and have only seen him in passing."

"It's a good thing too," Oslan added, "all he knows of the real you is an announcement I made when you first joined us that I would be training a new mage. He approved the idea and dismissed me so quickly he didn't even take the time to ask for your name." Oslan had been watching the king during the ball, and he knew that his father had not taken his eyes off them since they had begun to dance. This time, it seemed, he was interested. They reached the bottom of the stairs and stopped. The king nodded to the girl, and Oslan presented her. "Your Majesty, this is Aylan Suresword." Oslan bowed slightly, and when the vision didn't move, he hesitated. He held his bow longer than necessary, waiting for Aylan to follow suit. People started to notice the lack in etiquette and a soft murmur started up in places amongst the crowd.

"Bow, bow!" Lazelan urged.

"Girls don't bow!" Aylan argued.

"Curtsey then! Hurry!" Lazelan suggested frantically as the king began to look puzzled. The woman in blue at Oslan's side curtseyed then. It was deep and low and graceful, impressing them all. Only a noble who had been trained for years would carry themselves as she did, and the king breathed a sigh of relief.

"Aylan," the king began, "My son seems to have taken a fancy to you."

"And I to him," she replied in a gentle voice. The sound was music to Oslan's ears as he made it look as though he took the illusion's hand.

"Father, I wish for us to be married," he declared, "I trust that this vision of pure perfection agrees with you, unlike my previous choice."

The king glanced over at the girl in the tunic and hose that had given his son the token on the battlefield. She appeared to be glaring daggers at this newfound beauty. He could scarcely blame her, but she would find another, there had to be *someone* out there fit for such a girl, it just wouldn't be his son. "I believe that this is a much better choice." Eurilas agreed. "It is almost time for the *Endalwynndale Enchantment*; we shall seal the engagement with the toast!"

Slyly, the illusion murmured to Oslan: "He has no idea just how enchanted this evening has been!"

Thornton came out then with his lute and

started to strum the first chords of the song that always accompanied a toast and ended every feast and special occasion in their kingdom. The song called the *Endalwynndale Enchantment* had been commissioned by the king for his wedding day, and it now felt fitting to him that this would be the song playing as he announced the engagement of his son. Recorders and a drum came in and Thornton started to sing out in a ringing voice that carried across the hall:

"Twas long ago I first observed the dark eyes of a beauty,
I asked if I could escort her, as was my princely duty,
She tipped her head, gave her consent, and let me take her home,
She had my heart right from the start, and never have I roamed."

Before the second verse, there was a musical interlude, allowing the king enough time to ask after the lady's family. "My aunt is the Countess of Eshenberg," she replied truthfully.

"Indeed," the king said, pleased, "this *is* a much better choice, son. I welcome you into our family with open arms." The king announced to the illusion. The song continued as servers began to bring wine out from the kitchen to serve the guests for the toast. Thornton sang on as people's goblets were filled,

"Our visits were all chaperoned, as was the custom proper,
But she desired just one kiss, the chaperones couldn't stop her,
She threw her arms around my neck, a kiss to give my cheek,
And yet I swear it wasn't that that made my knees grow weak."

Thornton grinned and winked at the royal couple before starting heartily into the chorus:

"It was her eyes, her smile, her face, that truly took my heart,
I must admit there were those lips, that also did their part,
But in the end it was her words that filled my heart with pride,

'Twas when she said she'd stay with me, and still she's by my side."

By the close of the song, everyone present had a glass except the illusion. "I am afraid that I must decline," she said politely, and after planting a soft, careful kiss on Oslan's cheek, she continued: "I must keep a clear head when around such a handsome young man," she added to the approval of Eurilas.

The kiss had been so much like the one that the queen had given him so many years ago, that the king, already feeling nostalgic due to the song, was convinced that the two were as made for each other as the queen was for himself. He raised his glass and addressed the room: "Lords and Ladies, I have an auspicious announcement to make. My son has chosen a bride," the king intoned excitedly. "I present to you Aylan Suresword, my son's new fiancée." Everyone drank to the news and clapped, though some young ladies and their mothers did so forlornly. After the toast, the girl spoke again: "I am afraid that I must go now, Sire, I am already too late." She said to excuse herself.

"Well don't stand there son, accompany the lady home!" Eurilas encouraged. With a slight bow and a smile, Oslan walked the vision to the door, whereby it disappeared through the doorway from whence it came. Lazelan and Aylan quickly followed, releasing the crowd from the energy spell as they left.

Moments later, the king began to cough.

Chapter 35
~ Class and Glass ~

Tanyan found them celebrating in the gardens. They were having a good laugh at Aylan's line about the enchanting evening. "You know what this means now, don't you?" Sasha asked.

"That I actually get to marry for love?" Oslan answered.

"I was going to say that Aylan is going to have to learn to walk in ladies' shoes." Sasha cooed.

"Wouldn't you rather have the beauty that was on your arm tonight?" Lazelan jabbed, "It can be arranged you know."

Aylan gave him a playful sock on the arm as they heard a stricken voice interrupt:

"Oslan, it's Father, come quick!" It was Tanyan and she was falling to pieces. The usually very put-together princess had lines of worry creasing her usually smooth forehead. Tears streamed down her ruddy cheeks as she grabbed Oslan's hand and tried to lead him inside.

"What has happened?" Lazelan asked, alarmed.

"Father has fallen and isn't moving, I think he might be dying. Please come quick, Oslan! Lazelan, Father would want you there too, perhaps you can do something to help!" she barked at them. She led her father's son and mage inside, and the ladies retired to their rooms to await whatever news would come.

*   *   *

Zaltreous waited impatiently for three days, checking his scrying mirror almost every hour when he was not in class. He longed to learn the fate of

Endalwynndale's king. During lessons, he was so anxious that Rebekkah even noticed and asked Magdolyn if she knew what was up.

"He hasn't said anything to me," replied Magdolyn quietly as the professor droned on.

Rebekkah regarded Zaltreous from two rows behind him where the pair sat in the brightly lit classroom of the university. Normally, Zaltreous would try to sit with the girls if he arrived after them. Today however, he had swooped into the class, not even looking for them before choosing a seat nearest to the door. Now he sat biting his usually well-kept nails down to ragged stubs.

"Ugh!" Rebekkah uttered, disgusted at the thin thread of saliva that connected the man's finger and mouth.

"Something really must be wrong," Magdolyn surmised, "He's never like this. Maybe I should talk to him, it's obvious that he's under some kind of pressure."

"You go right ahead," Rebekkah encouraged, "I'll wait right here."

"You could come too," Magdolyn begged.

"No thanks, he might touch me with those gooey fingers. I'm staying far out of arms reach. Besides," Rebekkah added, "I'm sure he'd be much happier if you two were alone!"

Magdolyn rolled her green eyes and rose out of her seat. She descended a few steps in the isle and tapped Zaltreous on the shoulder so he would uncross his legs. He looked up in surprise and proffered the seat next to him. He moved his legs, giving her room to pass by him to the next chair. "Forgive me for not sitting with you ladies," he apologized, "I had some other things on my mind."

"I can see that," she replied, motioning to his fingertips. "What's going on?"

Zaltreous unconsciously hid his hands by crossing his arms over his chest. "Nothing, nothing. I am just waiting for some news about my thesis," he lied smoothly. "I might be taking a journey soon."

"For your thesis?" Magdolyn asked. "What's it about?"

"I'm afraid I cannot divulge that until I know for certain that it has been successful. However," he added, "If it has been, I expect to return here a rich man. When I return, may I take you to dinner again?"

"Zaltreous," she intoned reluctantly, "You know that I am with Lazelan."

For now, my firey-haired beauty, for now. He thought, *but soon you will be mine. If you resist, well, I will make sure that my castle has a tower with a good lock.*

Out loud, he simply replied: "Of course."

*   *   *

It was later that afternoon that Zaltreous finally saw what he had been waiting for in the scrying glass. The people in Endalwynndale were gathered wearing black. Many people were crying, and children clung to their mother's skirts. Husbands supported their wives and vice versa. All the servants of the castle walked in a solemn parade of black cloth and tears. The royal family followed, the queen flanked by her daughters in the finest of black dresses, black veils in front of their faces. The prince, Lazelan, and lords and dukes carried a long wooden box. Atop the box was a carving of the king's coat of arms. Zaltreous' mirror was revealing a funeral procession for the former ruler. His black heart soared as he gathered the last bit of information that he needed. Looking upon the prince, he saw that the boy still wore no kingly crown. The throne was Zaltreous' for the taking.

Chapter 36
~ Into the Sunset ~

After the funeral, Oslan waited another three days to tell his mother that he was leaving. "I must go stop the evil that threatens us." He persisted as she cried, not wanting to lose her only son so soon after her husband.

"But you must stay and take your place as king. This kingdom needs a ruler." She pleaded.

"I will come back for you and for the crown, Mother; you are more than capable of running this country until my return." He rebutted.

"Oslan, please," she begged, "If you won't stay for me, then stay for Aylan! You can't leave your new fiancée behind!"

Oh, she won't be staying behind, but that will have to remain my little secret. Oslan thought as he stepped closer to the queen and took both of her hands in his. "I know that you worry for me, but I will be careful. I want my future with Aylan more than you know. But, we won't have a future, Mother, if we are ruled under the thumb of darkness. First I will free us from this threat, then I will have earned my place as the true ruler of this kingdom. I leave with Lazelan's ship on the morrow. Fear not, for I will have my friends to protect me and fight at my side. I go with archers to accompany me, and I will have bright magic on my side as well to fight against the dark. If it eases you, Carn will also accompany us. He will be an asset to us as a swordsman, and he has tracked the *Almatraek Dim* before. I promise you that I will return as swiftly as I can." With that, Oslan kissed his mother tenderly on the cheek and went to say goodbye to his sisters, secretly wondering if it would be the last time they met.

＊　　　＊　　　＊

Zaltreous methodically packed everything he would need for his journey across the seas. He had no need for potions and pills, he could find whatever he needed in his precious book. The thick dark brown volume sat on his desk, ready to be packed last. He pulled the two leather straps around the side of the *Almatraek Dim*, and buckled them securely on top. Then he placed the heavy tome in his backpack, hiding it under the black cloak that was rolled up on top. He had hired a vessel that would take him to Endalwynndale and armed men to protect the book. They were just a bit of insurance, he never trusted hired mercenaries as a rule.

He hefted his backpack so that he could carry it using both straps, and set off for Ethik's docks. He passed by his town's shops and houses, not lonely, but still lost in the thought that no one would be bidding him farewell. He stopped briefly at a blacksmith's shop to purchase an expensive looking wood and metal chest with a lock. Inside it was nothing but air, yet his mercenaries would guard it with their lives. *As long as they think that they are on board to protect something,* he reasoned, *my book will be safe against attackers that may challenge us.*

He reached the edge of town as the sun started to set on the sea's horizon before him. The golden shimmer of the water moved and sparkled as waves reflected the burning orb's decent into nighttime. He squinted against its brightness as his shoes clunked up the gangplank. Handing the heavy chest over to the nearest hired man, he ordered: "Make sure you watch over this carefully, this ship now carries a treasure that many a man has sought after at their own peril."

"Aye aye, Sir, we shall place it in the hold. We'll not let any harm come to it." The burly man said as he effortlessly carried it to a hatch that led below deck. They cast off the lines holding them to the shore, and began their journey to Endalwynndale, sailing off into the sunset.

*   *   *

While the ship carrying Zaltreous travelled with the wind to the West, the ship carrying Aylan travelled against it to the East. They were sailing into darkness, the sunset falling behind them. Oslan, Carn and Lazelan stood by her side, looking out over the railing of the ship, fascinated by the multitude of stars beginning to appear in the sky. Thorn sat in the bow of the ship watching some friendly sea creatures pace the boat. Sasha sat in a trance in the cabin, trying to determine how long their trip would take, and how it might end. High above the decks, Bowregard had contentedly taken up a position in the crow's nest to keep an eye out for danger ahead.

"Do they know you've taken it?" Carn asked in a rough voice.

"No. I spoke only to my father's...I mean *my* general, Ormond, about my plans. I could not let my family worry about losing such a treasure, when they already feared so much at the thought of losing me," Oslan replied in a low voice.

"I see you don't share the same sense of worry," Carn observed.

"Mother tried to make me stay by telling me I was to ascend the throne. If they are really ready for me to be king, then they must be willing to follow my decisions and be ready for me to wield this. It comes with the job, and is my right to carry as the next in the bloodline," Oslan shot back.

Carn only nodded as Aylan asked the obvious question: "Oslan, what have you done? What treasure have you risked losing?"

In response, Oslan unsheathed his sword and held it out for them to see.

In the ship's lamplight, the beautiful etchings of the dragon's fire insignia beamed up at them from its hilt.   On the wavy scale-like blade, the fire-breathing dragon raced along the length of the gleaming serrated sword.

Chapter 37
~ Cloaks and Daggers ~

Zaltreous had stopped the boat. He had discovered on the first night that the boat's rolling and tossing from sea swells and waves did not make for a good night's sleep. Unfortunately for a mage, a lack of sleep resulting in a loss of concentration did not bode well. On the second night, Zaltreous ordered the ship to shore on a small scrap of land that could barely be called an island. He had slept well on dry land, and had ordered the crewman to drop anchor and row them to shore each night thereafter. This was the fourth night of their journey and a cooking fire was burning away, giving off sweet smells of wood smoke and meat that they had hunted in the sizable forest. The men sat around swapping stories of brawls gone by while they drank from the barrels of ale they had brought for the journey. A wild boar turned on a spit as its falling juices made the flames lick higher and sizzle.

*   *   *

Sasha warned them that they were getting close and Bowregard saw it first. Initially, it was only smoke in the distance. He called to a sailor for a spyglass to get a closer look. They passed up a telescope which he extended and brought to his eye. Sure enough, he could see the outline of a ship beside a body of land thick with trees. Flames flicked intermittently in and out of site as if being blocked by someone or something. He scurried down the rigging in order to pass on what he had seen. Aylan retrieved a bowl from the ship's cabin and asked that it be filled. A sailor returned it to her complete with swirling sea water. She placed it on the deck and her friends peered in around her. "Vearta uta da Ey seche ot isa. Vearta so baule viletla." *Reveal that which I seek to see. Reveal the island forest.*

When the swirling halted, they saw a clearing in the forest. On the outskirts of the clearing, there lay several bedrolls, a tent, and a chest with a lock flanked by two men. In the foreground was the band of men laughing and drinking around the fire. There were thirteen in all, including the lean figure that reclined against his backpack picking at his meat. "The book is in his bag." Sasha stated surely.

"Are you certain?" asked Thorn, "I'd wager that he's got it locked in that chest. It would be more secure."

"The bag is the only thing he has that's large enough to contain it. He would never let it out of his sight, nor would he leave it out of reach," Carn informed them. "It has a certain power over each owner: it makes them greedy to have it with them at all times."

"I can't even imagine an inanimate object having that kind of power over someone that is supposed to have free will," Bowregard shuddered.

"His will is free enough," concluded Carn, "It only feeds into the greed that is already there." They memorized the layout of the camp, the place where the rowboat was pulled up on the shore, and took note of the weaponry in their line of sight. When they had gotten all the information they could glean from scrying, Aylan dropped the spell and waited with Sasha on deck while the men went beneath to don their armour.

"You should stay here." Aylan advised her friend.

"You know I can't just sit here and watch." Sasha protested, "If something were to happen to any of you I would at least want the chance to help."

Aylan sighed and removed a leather satchel. She opened the top flap to reveal a multitude of packets inside. "I thought you might say that. I've made these for you. They're all labeled, so make sure you know what you're throwing before you use them." Sasha took the bag gratefully. She closed the flap, secured it, and ducked into the strap so it fell diagonally from shoulder to opposite hip.

"As for myself," Sasha added, "I promise to avoid any attacks. I will know of them before they come at me." Aylan smiled in relief.

Lazelan needed no armour. Instead, he emerged from the cabin in a velvety red-wine coloured cape with golden suns that blazed down the trim. It had a large hood with which he could shade his face, and it reached all the way to the floor. He approached Aylan and gave her a small bundle tied with a silver gossamer ribbon. "I was going to give this to you when I left, thinking you might have use for it someday. I am sorry that it had to be so soon."

Aylan unwrapped the bundle to find a similar cloak inside, but this one was navy blue velvet and had silver stars that shimmered along the trim. At the throat, the clasp was a silver copy of the fire breathing insignia of Endalwynndale. Tears glistened in her eyes as she swung the beautiful garment around her and fastened the clasp. "Oh Lazelan, it's beautiful!" she gushed reverently, "How can I ever thank you?"

"Use it to protect yourself and the future king. I have taught you and you have learned well. Do your job to its fullest, and most importantly of all," he added somberly, "don't die tonight." She tried to hug him then, and found that she could not. A barrier blocked her when she tried to go near him.

"You didn't think it was just a pretty garment, did you?" Lazelan teased. "It is infused with a magical and physical shield. While opened, spells and objects can penetrate in and out, when closed, even an advanced spell will have trouble having its full effect on you. Beware though, should it be torn, a hole will appear in your shield as well, so be on guard."

A short while later, the knights joined them, dressed from head to toe in their full battle gear. The two knights-in-training wore the studded leather armour of their archery outfits to help them move more easily than bulkier metal suits would allow. They bore metal chest plates and bucklers, and hard leather bracers for protection while shooting. Across their backs they also wore their quivers, which were filled with carefully made arrows. Bowregard still wore the old armour of a training knight despite his winning the archery contest, as the king had died before making him a knight. "If we get through this", said Thorn fearfully to the prince, "will you make us both knights before the night is through?" The friends silently pitied the terrified boy as they regarded him with his quiver on his back and his father's too large bow in hand.

In answer, Oslan's armour clanged softly as he nodded his assent and gave the boys the kingdom's salute.

Chapter 38
~ Going Head to Head,
(To head, to head, to head) ~

Lazelan and Aylan worked together to shield their small rowboat from detection while using magic to move them quickly and quietly through the water. Each member of their party carried a small packet to prevent them from being scried by the enemy. They reached the island on the opposite shore from the camp and disembarked. With their feet sinking into the soft sand of the beach, and the full moon above to light their way, they headed inland toward the row of trees that marked the beginning of the island's vegetation. They wandered through the lush expanse of forest until the sound of the waves lapping at the shore grew faint and they began to hear the first hints of voices and merry making ahead. Then, at Carn's hand signal, they began to fan out into the foliage to be able to take their foes from more than one side. As silently as possible, Bow and Thorn each nocked an arrow and drew back slightly on their bow strings, readying their shots. Aylan flanked Oslan, and Lazelan stayed with Carn, walking in front of Sasha both for protection and to offer healing should one of the members of their band fall. Tension mounted as they drew closer to what would be a first real battle for most of them. Each little skittering sound in the forest only served to make them feel edgier. The wind in the trees was a distraction. Then a false movement as Thorn looked up to see a scurrying squirrel jump from tree limb to tree limb. "Watch out!" Sasha hissed, as Thorn, distracted by the small animal, stepped on an old fallen tree branch. The *crack* rang out through the darkness and conversation in the camp cut off.

"I'm sorry Carn!" he started to apologize, but Carn cut him off with a shushing finger held in front of his visor. He pointed up to the trees, and Sasha and the two bowmen began to climb. Aylan and the rest continued to advance more quickly now, not needing to be quiet as the soldiers in the camp collected weapons and made ready for a fight.

"Ten of them will come down the path, two will stay behind to protect the chest we saw," Sasha warned them.

Many of the hired thugs did not take the time to put on armour, but only grabbed their weapons and charged into the forest to do battle. As the bands clashed together, the clang of swords rang out, occasionally followed by Skirdkhen's hiss of fire. Fire packets rained down from Sasha's tree, creating bursts of light that the archers could use to see their targets all the more clearly. The mercenaries were trained, but unprepared. They had grown soft on drink and their movements were slow and clumsy. They fell and fell and fell. Bowregard proved to be just as accurate a shot on these targets as in the arena, and took out a soldier that had tried to sneak up on Oslan.

Without having fired one shot, Thorn let out a frightened "Help!" from his place in the crook of a tree branch. Only ten feet below him, another mercenary had sheathed his sword and was currently scaling the tree, a dagger in his mouth. Aylan called upon the same force she had used to move Scritch the imp, but now more powerful, she was able to dislodge the big man and send him falling into a bush. Eventually, no more men came. No one had seen Zaltreous or the book since the beginning of the fray, and the band from Endalwynndale regrouped on the ground so that they could form a plan of some sort to find him and deal with the two that still guarded the chest.

In the middle of the discussion, Sasha went silent, and then suddenly exclaimed: "Watch out for their four heads!"

"Foreheads? What could they possibly do with their foreheads?" Thorn asked.

Before Sasha could correct him, the ground began to shake at even intervals, and the sound of trees' roots being ripped out of the ground filled the night. *Trees are being uprooted and are crashing to the forest floor, but how?* Aylan pondered as the ground shook beneath her. *Has Zaltreous found a way to make earthquakes swallow us up, or a tornado to fling us all into the sea? That can't be it, there is no wind,* she reasoned. Then a sound ripped through their heads and bodies so loudly that they could feel it pulsing through them. It was a terrific bestial cry let loose to the stars above. They all covered their ears to keep them from being deafened as the creature continued to bellow.

They rushed forward at the sounds of men yelling: "Stay back!" and finally reached the clearing. The two soldiers that had remained with the chest screamed and ran away together in fear, but not from Aylan's party of friends. Zaltreous was temporarily forgotten as the magnificent sight of the deadly red and black four-headed creature raged in front of them. Its feet created thunder whenever it moved a leg. Its tail, swishing in anger, made the clearing larger as it destroyed more forest with every swipe. It was as tall as the trees, and its mighty wings unfolded and flapped in anger.

"What is it?" Thorn shouted above the terrible din.

"A dragon," Lazelan replied wisely, "Zaltreous must have used the book to summon it."

"Why does it behave so?" questioned Bow,

"We haven't done anything to it!"

"It doesn't wish to be here," Lazelan reported, "it is under Zaltreous' power, and will continue to rampage until it is set free. Beware its heads, they all have the ability to attack with more than its teeth, and each can be deadly and different."

As if on cue, the dragon's second head snapped forward, sending out a burst of yellow and orange flame thirty feet long and as tall as a man. Oslan stepped in front of Aylan and raised his shield as the tip of the burst of flames came at him. They licked around the edge of his shield, threatening to burn him. As the fire continued, the paint on his shield began to peel and melt away and the metal started to change colour to a bright hot red. Aylan cast a spell that sent a cooling bubble around them, and protected the arm holding Oslan's shield. Suddenly, the flame burst stopped, and the dragon let out another screech of frustration. Lazelan began a new incantation, and when he was done, the dragon seemed to be stomping it's feet less and folded its wings back into place along its hard shell of scales.

"What happened?" Thorn asked, "What did he do?"

Aylan replied to this question with a hint of awe in her voice: "he calmed it down".

"It's not over yet!" cautioned Sasha, "Get ready to hold your breath!"

Just then from behind the dragon came a blaze of light. A white ball of magic heat shot through the right wing of the dragon and it started to bellow once more. This time, each of its heads spurted a different substance at random. Flames shot again into the air, as did an acid so potent that it ate away a crater in the dirty earth wherever it hit.

A noxious gas filled the air and as the last head let out a mighty scream, the small band of friends once again felt the sound tear through them, their molars left vibrating in their gums. Lazelan conjured a wind that cleared the air of the dangerous gases, allowing them to breathe once more.

Bowregard raised his bow and shot in defense. The result was a dull *tock* and *snap!* As the arrow hit the dragon on its scaly shoulder and splintered, each piece ricocheted off without leaving a mark. The dragon started to advance upon them now seeing them as a threat. Each step caused the ground to shake, and it began to ready its heads to unleash yet another volley of attacks, this time all directed at their band. Closer and closer the dragon thundered. Carn moved to cover Lazelan and Oslan simply reached out for Aylan's hand. He raised his shield once more as the dragon took a final step. *Thwap!*

A decidedly human howl filled the air then as the dragon stopped its onslaught. It paused and reared up onto its hind legs, front feet pawing the air. It took a moment to test its wings before deciding that it could still fly despite the small injury Zaltreous' magic had made to its right wing. It rose up into the night sky with six flaps of its mighty wings before flying off in a direction presumably toward its home.

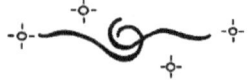

Chapter 39
~ The Worth of a Crown ~

Dumbfounded, all members of the band from Endalwynndale turned toward Thorn. After a minute of silence in which Thorn scuttled to the ground, they converged on him, hugging him and congratulating him on his fine shot.

"That was quick thinking to shoot at the mage," Bow remarked.

"I just remember thinking about how Millie said it's easy for Aylan to lose a spell if she is distracted. I thought maybe I could distract him enough to set the dragon free," Thorn explained. "I saw Zaltreous' cloak hanging open as he held the book in front of him. I wasn't really sure that the dragon wouldn't try to eat us anyway," he admitted glumly, "I took a chance on all of our lives."

"And you'll do it again," Carn announced as he clapped him on the back. "That's the life of a hero. Gambles and luck with a little skill thrown in! Now let's go catch us a mage."

Behind the giant footprints left by the dragon, they saw a path leading back into the trees. They would have to continue single file to move quickly along the trail in order to catch up.

"He won't be moving too fast with an injury from Thorn's arrow," Carn advised, "besides, that book weighs a ton."

The six brave friends rushed through the forest, searching for a sign of the evil mage ahead. As they ran along the path, Carn in front followed by the rest, it didn't escape their notice that the birds had ceased to sing. Even allowing that they may have been snuggled in their expertly made nests for the night, there should have been some nocturnal scurrying or even the regal hoot of an owl.

But the forest around them had grown silent; their clanging footfalls were the only sounds to be heard. Oslan and Carn were both aware of the sound of their own heavy breathing inside their visored helmets as they carried the heavy suits of armour forward on their bodies. The prince's silvery armour shone in the moonlight, his family's crest clear on his chest plate. Carn's armour resounded and his helmet's fringe of blue fur rustled softly as he ran. The two archers followed behind them, Thorn with his father's longbow and Bowregard with his own. Lazelan and Aylan brought up the rear behind Sasha, so they would have some kind of defenses should one of the scared mercenaries come upon them from behind.

"Duck!" Sasha screamed. In front of the throng there was a sudden *smack,* followed by a sizzling sound as a bright orb of white light came flying back down the trail from up ahead. It smashed into a tree a meager two feet from Carn's head, disintegrating the bark and eating into the side of the tree causing a wild flash that burned into all of their eyes, then winked out into darkness.

"Down!" Carn shouted as he dodged away from the injured tree. They all rolled and crawled away into the underbrush in order to find cover. Lazelan ordered Aylan to stay down, but he himself stood and began to pace forward while making sure that his cloak was securely closed in front of him.

"Lazelan, old friend," a voice only familiar to Lazelan and Sasha began, "I was afraid I might never see you again. This is a pleasant surprise."

"I wish I could say the same Zaltreous, but you just tried to kill my friend," he retorted.

They could hear a dark chuckling come from somewhere up ahead. "Oh Lazelan, Lazelan, I did no such thing," he said brightly, "If I had wanted him dead, he would no longer be breathing. I just wanted the two of us to have some space to...talk," he finished congenially. Just as the last word fell on their ears, another orb of light burst through the trees and hit Lazelan's cloak square in the chest. There was a burst of light once more, and it faded, yet there was no trace on the cloak that anything had befallen it.

"I'm sorry Zaltreous, could you repeat that last bit, I couldn't hear you over the sound of your spell failing," Lazelan jibbed.

Zaltreous took a few steps closer to his foe. Now they were just visible to each other along the path. "Hmm, I forgot about that old cloak," came the reply. "Oh well, onward and upward," he continued. He turned, his own black cape billowing out behind him revealing a bloody stain on his side before he disappeared. Thudding foot falls could be heard ahead as he padded away up the path once more.

"After him!" Carn commanded, rising from his place in order to follow Zaltreous. Lazelan put a hand on his arm in order to stop him from advancing.

"We have seen that he has crossed the darkest of lines. He is not above killing to obtain his goals. We must proceed with caution." Lazelan advised.

"Agreed. We will proceed from different directions as before. Archers, ready your bows, but do not show yourselves, stick to the underbrush. You don't want to make yourselves a target," Carn declared. "Lazelan, with these cloaks that you mages wear, is there any way for us to pass his defenses?"

"Just one," Lazelan affirmed, "There is a rip

in the back of his cloak where Thorn's arrow must have passed through after finding its mark."

The group spread out to chase their quarry once more. Up the path into the night they hunted, wary of more attacks. Finally, they saw a growing light ahead. The trees started thinning, and they reached another expanse of land that offered little to no cover. This clearing was smaller than the one that had housed the bon fire, but this one seemed to be in an older part of the forest. Here, the trees were mossy and so stout that a grown man would have found it a challenge to wrap his arms fully around one. On the other side of the clearing, Zaltreous knelt with the *Almatraek Dim* open on his lap. His hands gave off a bright red light as he mumbled to himself in Almatrae, incanting something from the book.

*   *   *

Zaltreous watched as the two archers took positions on either side of the path, using a couple of large trees for cover. Lazelan and a lady with blond hair, both wearing cloaks, stepped into the clearing, with two knights on either side of them. He saw the crown over the crest on the chest plate of one suit of armour, and recognized that as a symbol of royalty. *So,* he thought elated, *it seems as though I need not wait any longer. I can finish this here, since they have brought the prince right to me. The one with the blue fringe must be his hired guard. No matter, that one won't last long.* At that, Zaltreous raised his glowing right hand and pointed it at Aylan. "This must be your little protégé," Zaltreous guessed, let me see how well you've trained her."

"I wouldn't do that if I were you," Lazelan warned, "she is the prince's fiancée. If you raise a hand to her, be warned, that you will be tried for crimes against the crown when we return to Endalwynndale."

"We wouldn't want that now, would we?" Zaltreous mocked as he moved and flicked his wrist, instead sending a blast of ice shooting toward the inconsequential guard. He watched as the knight dodged the shot, only barely, and ran off into the woods to avoid another without even drawing his sword. "You just can't trust hired help," Zaltreous quipped.

He moved to aim once again at the girl, remarking that she was pretty. *It's almost a shame to have to kill her, but I can't have her opposing me.* He argued with himself, lost in thought. Two blasts of light struck Zaltreous' cloak, knocking him back a few steps. He remained uninjured, but had lost his spell. He quickly started to recast another, but was unable to finish by the time Lazelan had closed his cloak after the pair's attacks. Luckily for Zaltreous though, Lazelan's apprentice was not as fast as he. Zaltreous shot a purple bolt at Aylan, hitting her full force. The bolt turned green as it surrounded her in a floating bubble. He said another incantation and held his free hand up as if to stop them.

Inside her bubble and determined to get out, Aylan began to chant. "Do not cast Aylan!" Lazelan called to her in warning, "In your prison, the spell will bounce back onto you, and have a worse effect." Frustrated, and feeling helpless, Aylan dropped the spell and waited. The two archers, hidden by the trees, each let an arrow fly. There was a small packet secured to each tip, and as they stopped in mid-air, a foot from Zaltreous' hand, they both burst into flames and burned as if thrown up against an invisible wall.

"Nice trick," Zaltreous complimented them.

Then turning to the crested armour, he continued: "You have quite a resourceful group of friends, Your Highness. Now, I suggest that you disarm yourself and swear fealty to me as your new king."

"And why would he want to do that?" Lazelan scoffed, "You have no power over him, and both of your hands are busy. All he has to do is draw his sword and run you through. At the very least, you'll have to set Aylan free."

As if on cue, the figure reached across the armour's crest and drew his sword, the sound ringing out in the dark.

"On the contrary," he argued, "I have all the power. Drop your sword, Prince of Endalwynndale, or I shall fill this Aylan's bubble with poisoned gas. I can assure you that I can make it as painful as I want. You wouldn't want your betrothed to die in convulsions like your father now, would you?" Zaltreous challenged despicably. "Now drop your sword, surrender your kingdom to me and kneel!" he commanded.

"No, don't!" Aylan yelled to Oslan in horror. Conflicted between the thought of losing the freedom of the kingdom to this maniac if the prince disarmed himself, or losing their happy future if she was to die here and now, she made a difficult decision and tried to plead with him. "I'm not worth it Oslan. Think of all the lives of the families living in Endalwynndale that *you* are responsible for! I don't want to live if this is what we have to go back to."

Her words seemed to fall however on deaf ears. The sword fell to the forest floor with a muffled thud. The shining suit of armour's crest dipped as it bent at the knee and hip, and knelt in front of the foe.

Zaltreous cackled in triumph as he flung the spell holding Aylan as far as he could. The bubble carried her across the clearing where it burst against a tree trunk. Aylan cried out at the impact her body made against the rough bark, and fell to the ground silent and unmoving. Lazelan pursed his lips as Sasha rushed to her side.

Zaltreous felt the heat from the sword's blade seconds before it touched his back. With a quick intake of breath, he fumbled the book in surprise and clutched at it with both hands, causing his cloak to fall opened further. From behind him, he heard a commanding voice warn him, "You better not have hurt my fiancée. She is not a lady to be trifled with."

"But who? How?" Zaltreous had time to wonder as he stared at the still kneeling prince, powerless before him. Then he was surrounded by a flash of blue light as Aylan, now on her feet, hit him with her own encasing spell. Lazelan walked up to the blue bubble and regarded his old friend.

"Did Maggie not tell you that she was a fast learner?"

Understanding finally unclouded Zaltreous' mind as the prince before him once again rose to his feet. His gauntleted hands reached up to slowly remove his royal helmet, revealing not the face of the prince, but that of a stranger. The blond haired man approached the bubble, sword now back in hand, and asked Aylan to drop the spell that was holding the mage. "My name is Carn, and after a long search, this book now belongs to me," he said. As soon as the spell was gone, Carn reached out and plucked the book from Zaltreous' unwilling hands.

"Good news," the real prince shared with Zaltreous, still behind his back, "Sasha tells us that you wanted a tower with a good lock. It just so happens that my kingdom has one and you will find yourself in it quite soon."

Chapter 40
~ Trials and Treaties ~

After removing Zaltreous' protective cloak and casting a spell on him that would prevent him from using magic, the party from Endalwynndale bore him and the book back to their ship. He was locked in the brig below deck, where Lazelan and Carn remained to guard him by magic and sword. Bowregard and Thornton stood before Oslan under the sails and starry sky. Asking them to kneel, he explained that though they were now being knighted, an official ceremony in front of the court would follow once he was crowned king, so they could be presented to the kingdom as having finally earned their fire. They returned home as heroes, with bells sounding and people gathered on the docks to welcome them back. As they disembarked, Millie met them at the gangplank. She first hugged Aylan, and then walked to Bowregard, giving him a kiss that lasted until the rest were off the ship.

In the weeks that followed, much took place. Lazelan returned with his friends to Ethik and to a very excited Magdolyn. He was thrown immediately into arrangements for his wedding, and as Bowregard, and Thorn helped to plan and purchase what he needed, Sasha and Millie worked with Rebekkah to pick flowers for bouquets, find a tailor to make Maggie's dress and buy ribbons for her hair. Aylan and Oslan stayed at the manor and met with the Earl of Ethik to strike up an accord. A new peace treaty was written and signed that allowed for safe trade and travel among the two realms. Within a couple of weeks, Lazelan and Magdolyn stood between Oslan and Rebekkah as they were joined in marriage before the people of Ethik. It seemed as though the whole town had come out to watch, and the resulting party seemed to go on for days, filling the pubs and inns with merry making. As Bowregard and Millie danced together in one such tavern, Bow ventured to ask her if she thought he would make a good husband. "I can't answer for anyone else here," she boldly told him, "but I think you would make a fine husband for me." He kissed her then and it was settled. Thorn became very popular with the young ladies of Ethik as they flocked around him to hear him sing and play. "You know," the prince remarked to Lazelan as they listened and shared a mug of ale, "perhaps his path is to become a bard." Indeed, by the time the week was through, Thorn's purse-strings were heavy and the *Endalwynndale Enchantmen* was on everyone's lips.

Once the celebrations were through and the friends bade farewell to one another, they began their journey by ship back home. Settling back into castle life, Oslan began to take on more of a kingly role. Though he first had to marry, he prepared with his mother for his impending coronation by holding court, meeting with Ormond, and listening to peasants that came to speak to him about matters of state.

Aylan and Sasha spent quite a bit of time together picking herbs in the forest and transforming Lazelan's old laboratory into Aylan's own. A visit to the marketplace supplied them with more candles and wall sconces to allow for more light as she worked. Finally, the two ladies travelled to the tailor to arrange for a surprise for Millie. They picked out some beautiful lace and expensive fabric and handed them over to the small man with the measuring tape strung around his neck. This was to be their wedding present to Millie. It would be a new dress in the style of the yellow one that had been so becoming on her, but dove white to mark her purity on her special day.

Zaltreous was removed from the tower dungeon where he had been awaiting trial. Judgment was passed, and he was returned to the tower indefinitely. Some folks had called for his head, however, Oslan argued that he should live. The prince figured that he may be of some use in learning more about the *Almatraek Dim* and its sister, the *Almatraek Bright*, which he intended to one day track down.

Zaltreous' tower dungeon was set apart from the rest, so he was ensured to be completely alone. His only window was bricked in, so that he could not cast on people that he might look down upon. The two door guards were afforded magic cloaks of their own, so they would be unsusceptible to any magic he might try to use on them to free himself. As a final precaution, packets were created and sealed into the brickwork all along the walls of his prison that would continually zap his internal power, leaving him able to function as a normal person, but unable to build up the energy necessary to cast even the smallest spell.

Chapter 41
~ Magic Moment ~

Now as before, Oslan waited impatiently for Aylan to appear. He paced back and forth past the tapestries in the hall just inside the castle's large balcony that overlooked the square. Talithan, Tanyan and Trindalynn had taken Aylan hostage, and Millie had expressly forbidden him from seeing her all day. *Will I ever understand this?* He wondered as he passed Carn and the other guards on duty for the two hundredth time. *All she has to do is put on a dress!* Millie finally came bustling down the hall wearing a smile as broad as her face would allow. "Now close your eyes, she's coming!" Millie commanded.

He turned to Carn for help, but before he could protest, there came a soft click-clicking of dainty shoes on the marble floor. They all gazed down the hall as Millie harrumphed in defeat. Striding steadily toward them was the girl from the ball. Her sculpted bodice and flowing gown was identical except that now it was the light turquoise of the favour Aylan had given him at the tournament. He could scarcely believe his eyes, and meant to complain that instead of just putting on a dress, she had created this charade again.

When he heard a familiar swish of the material as she drew nearer, he was convinced of the illusion, though the sound of the shoes as well was impressive. More remarkable was the faint scent of lilacs that rose from her skin as she came closer. *She really has gotten better at this,* was the thought that ran through his mind. She reached for his hand and he instinctively took it, shocked that it felt so warm and real. Knowing she could hear him through the illusion, he questioned her "Why didn't you just put on a dress?" He stood looking at the lady before him, wondering how the illusion's eyes could be so much like Aylan's real ones, when they slid closed and she kissed him softly and fully on the lips.

Instantly, the familiar feeling of her kiss made the realization hit home for him. *She did put on a dress, it's really her!* he reflected, elated. He had always thought her pretty, and he supposed that over the past year that opinion had changed slightly. He realized that her freckles had faded and her hair had grown out. His hands rose up to hold her face as he savored the moment, and as he cupped her jaw-line, he realized that it had lost its roundness in favour of the more angular lines of a woman. All she had been missing all along was the dress to complete her transformation into a lady from the girl that she had once been.

Regretfully, feeling it was too soon, he ended the kiss and stepped back. "You really are magical," he breathed. "It is time now, everyone is waiting. Are you ready to have your secret revealed?" As butterflies once more made her stomach churn, she nervously nodded her consent and allowed the knights on guard to precede them outside. She boldly took the crown prince's hand to lend her strength and took a deep, shaky breath as they turned to the curtains before them.

A cheer erupted from the adoring peasantry below as minutes later, the couple stepped out onto the balcony together to tell the world that Aylan was a mage.

~ The End of Book One ~

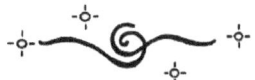

Dear Adventurer,

Thank you for coming along as we begin our journey through the vast and sometimes perilous kingdom of Endalwynndale. I hope you have found a character to side with, and have been brave as you shared in their joy, sorrow, love or excitement. I have enjoyed writing about this wondrous world, and I sincerely hope that you have had as much fun in discovering its enigmas as I have. I hope you will return soon, and will join us on our voyage in the sequel, *Noble Pursuit*, where Oslan will uncover hidden secrets from Aylan's past, and will be forced to risk life and limb to recapture his kingdom from a new and even more dangerous threat.

Till A Quest Calls Again,

Heather Reilly

P.S. If you have enjoyed this tale, the biggest compliment you could give me would be to recommend this book to another person. Word of mouth is a powerful thing, and you can help to get the story out there.